A Strange High
—A Strange Portent

Laurie found himself in a small, sparsely furnished, single ward. The furnishings were minimal and consisted of a white metal bed, a metal locker and a wash basin. Lying on the bed, curled up in a foetal position, was a girl of about sixteen.

The girl's huge eyes were wide open but he sensed that they were not seeing him at all. He glanced around and, as he did so, something struck him sharply just below his right ear. He gave a grunt of surprise, jerked upright, and a flexible, pink plastic mug fell to the floor at his feet.

The girl did not even blink. Wherever she was, it was apparently too far away for words to reach her. Yet she was alive, and in a curious way Laurie sensed that she *was* watching them, tucked away deep inside herself like some wary little forest animal.

Richard Cowper

TIME OUT OF MIND

PUBLISHED BY POCKET BOOKS NEW YORK

*"Time present and time past
Are both perhaps present in time future
And time future contained in time past."*
                        T. S. ELIOT *Burnt Norton*

POCKET BOOKS, a Simon & Schuster division of
GULF & WESTERN CORPORATION
1230 Avenue of the Americas, New York, N.Y. 10020

ISBN: 0-671-83580-7

First Pocket Books printing January, 1981

Originally published in Great Britain in 1973 by
Victor Gollancz Ltd.

10 9 8 7 6 5 4 3 2 1

POCKET and colophon are trademarks of Simon & Schuster.

Printed in the U.S.A.

The boy picked his way among the water-worn rocks at the river's edge, the scarlet-tipped float tap-tapping against the mottled cane shaft of the fishing rod he gripped in his right hand. Although dawn was already some two hours past the sun had only just thrust itself above the eastern mountains and frail cobwebs of mist were still rising among the branches of the riverside trees.

He knew exactly where he was going—the bend where the current had scoured out a long dark overhang among the oak roots and where, the previous year, he had hooked and lost the biggest trout he had ever seen. For ten months now that monstrous fish had haunted his day-dreams and he knew, as only the born fisherman *can* know, that it was still there, waiting for him.

He scrambled over a granite slab, slid gingerly down to a ridge of pebbles, skipped over a swirling, peat-stained pool and gained the shoulder of firm sand that sloped away into the bight of the bend. He stood still for a moment while his brown eyes flickered from point to point, noting the differences a winter had brought—a tangle of dead grass and twigs hooked high up in the trailing branches of the oak; some new holes burrowed into the subsoil by the water's edge; a bristling spruce trunk, bleached bone-white by the June sun, which must have been dragged down from the forestry plantations at the head of the valley by the spring floods.

He now became very cool and methodical. So often had he rehearsed this moment in his imagination that he was able to contain his mounting excitement and was aware of it only as a sort of hollow feeling in his stomach, a tenseness in his chest. Keeping well back from the hurrying water he made his way stealthily across the sand bank and scrambled up into a shallow depression in the rocks. This hollow was, in fact, the lip of a gulley, overgrown with brambles and elder down which, during the winter storms, flash water from the hills drained into the main stream. Now it was a dry and shady tunnel, carpeted with a drifting of dead leaves, and it offered him excellent cover.

He unlooped the sling bag from his shoulder, set it down beside him, and unwound the nylon trace by the simple expedient of twitching the rod so that the float twirled round and did the job for him. Then he laid the rod carefully on the rocks, unbuckled the bag and took out the perforated tin which contained the worms he had brought for bait. Having selected one he snicked it on to the hook, thumbed off the ratchet on the reel, and taking hold of the trace in his left hand, swung out the rod tip, at the same moment releasing the trace.

The float swooped out, the black monofil line whispering off the spool, and he saw the cast drop precisely at the point he had intended. As the bait vanished beneath the scurrying, bubble-laced water, the boy let out his pent breath in a faint ecstatic sigh.

The float had travelled downstream no more than a dozen feet before it bobbed and plunged under. He struck sharply and felt the immediate, heart-stopping shock that told him he had hooked a fish. He checked its first panic rush and turned it so that it drove upstream away from the roots of the oak, then he reeled it in and hoisted it up on to the ledge. It rose, wriggling frenziedly and scattering glittering waterdrops over the cold rocks. A trout but not *the* trout. About half a pound. Three more like it and his mother could revise their supper menu. Frowning with concentration he grasped the fish firmly and banged its head against the rock. It twitched once and its rosy gills fluttered and folded like petals against its speckled flanks. Then he removed the hook, laid the fish on one side, wiped his hands on a rag and prepared to re-bait.

He had just reached out towards the bait tin when he sensed that he was no longer alone. Years later, trying to recall what it was that had first alerted him, he wondered whether he had not heard some sound— the click of a breaking twig, the rasp of a bramble— but could recall nothing. Yet at that moment it was as if a cold hand had brushed across the nape of his neck. He felt the skin on his back and shoulders cringe; his hair stir. Very, very slowly he turned his head and peered over his right shoulder.

The man was half-squatting, half-kneeling in the shadowy tunnel of the gulley. He was dressed in a tightly fitting overall that looked black but might have been dark blue. There was a strip about an inch wide of some bright yellow metal banded across his forehead ending in two small gold spirals just above his temples. Two similar bands braceleted his wrists. As

7

soon as the boy's eyes alighted upon his, the man's lips moved, but no sound emerged.

The boy gaped, poised on the razor edge between terror and curiosity. There was something about the man, some quality of yearning so intense that it held his fear in check. "Who are you?" he whispered.

Again the dark eyes pleaded, the lips moved. But the boy heard nothing, no sound at all. And suddenly he noticed something else, something utterly incredible. A single thin shaft of the morning sunlight, probing through the tangled undergrowth, was striking the man's right shoulder and was apparently *passing right through him!* It fell like a tarnished sovereign on the dry, drifted leaves beyond his bent left knee.

At that same instant the trout gave a sudden galvanic shudder, flapped twice and lay still. The imperative reflex fear of losing his catch momentarily twitched the boy's attention away from the man. When he glanced back a second later his mysterious visitant was gone.

The boy peered around apprehensively. The sunbeam was still there, so where then was the man? Very slowly and cautiously he rose to his feet and gazed about him. Nothing was changed in any way. He looked down at the rod lying by his feet and then back to the gully. Impossible for anyone to have got out without being seen or heard: impossible for anyone to have got *in* either! *Could* he have imagined it? He squatted down again and squinted into the tunnel, then, with his heart racing madly, he shuffled gingerly forward for the four yards that separated him from the sunbeam and peered down at the ground. The dead leaves lay undisturbed where they had drifted. How *could* anyone have knelt there and left no trace? So what *had* he seen? A ghost? He scurried back to the rock ledge and, partly to reassure himself and partly because he was a child with a methodical mind,

8

he pushed back the cuff of his sweater and consulted the wrist chronometer which had been given to him on his thirteenth birthday a fortnight before. "Six twenty-seven," he said out aloud. "July the seventeenth, 1987." And then, unaccountably, he shivered.

The dark blue hovertruck with the silver lightning-bolt insignia edged its way up out of the concrete channel and skittered off up the valley toward the high dam. The man at the controls glanced back over his shoulder and said: "How is he, Doc?"

"Still out cold," replied the girl.

"He's O.K., though?"

"Pulse and respiration are both steady. Temperature's down a bit."

"Do you think it worked?"

"How do I know, Steve?"

"You know what I think, Billie? I think the whole idea's completely lunatic. But *crazy!* Shall I tell you why?"

The girl said nothing, seemingly preoccupied with removing the metal bracelets from the wrists of the unconscious man who lay slumped in a tilt chair at the back of the truck.

"For one thing your co-ordinates."

"What about them?"

"Well, they're relative not absolute."

"I'm not with you."

"It's the old flaw in all the time-travel stories. Nothing stands still. We're careering through space at 300 kilometers a second. Jump backward or forward even ten minutes and you'll likely find yourself in the void."

"No one's jumping anywhere," said the girl. "It's just a psychic energy field projection."

"You believe that?"

The hovertruck slid crabwise on to the macadam-

9

ized highway, settled and went into wheel drive. The girl succeeded in unfastening the second bracelet and slotted it alongside its companion in the purpose-molded foam lining of a plastic container. Then she set about detaching the band from the man's forehead. By the time that too had been stowed away and the container clipped shut the truck was rolling on to the roadway which traversed the top of the dam. At once the full stature of the engineering feat became apparent. The twin arms of the sail-dotted lake could be seen reaching out into the mountains northward till they vanished from sight in the blue distance.

The man called Steve took one hand off the controls and gestured across the water. "This must have been quite a place."

"What do you mean, 'Must have been?' " said the girl.

"When Laurie was a kid."

Hearing his name spoken the man in the chair groaned faintly and opened his eyes.

The girl bent over him solicitously. "Laurie? Are you feeling all right?"

The man's eyelids fluttered down and then up again. "Billie?"

"Here. Drink this." She dropped a pink tablet into a plastic cup, slopped some water on to it from a flask and swirled it round watching the tablet disintegrate in bubbles. The man lay passive, watching her, saying nothing.

"How do you feel?" she asked. "Numb?"

He nodded and ran his tongue along his lower lip.

"It'll wear off in a minute or two," she said. "How about the head?"

"Aches like hell," he whispered.

"What did you expect?" She grinned and held the cup to his lips.

He took a couple of sips, swallowed and closed his eyes again.

"No," she said firmly. "Finish it. Come on."

Steve called out: "I hate to be the bearer of unwelcome tidings but I have a sneaky suspicion someone's on to us."

The girl stretched her arm across the man in the chair, prised apart two slats of the venetian blind that shuttered the rear window and peered out. "You're dreaming, Steve," she said. "There's no one."

For answer Steve lifted the index finger and jerked it toward the truck's metal roof. "Look up there."

"Are you *sure?*"

"No," he admitted. "It's just a feeling."

The girl lifted one of the man's hands and pressed his fingers around the cup. "Go on," she urged. "Finish it. You'll feel better."

"I feel lousy," he mumbled.

"That's what I mean."

The man groaned, raised the cup to his lips and drained it off.

"Good," she said and scrambled up to the front of the truck. "Now show me, Steve."

The driver leaned forward and glanced upward through the domed perspex. "There."

She craned her neck and stared up at the little red and white craft which was floating like a seed of thistledown about a thousand feet above them. "How do you know it isn't an amenity patrol?" she said. "There must be hundreds of boats out there today."

"I don't *know,*" he said. "Like I said it's just a feeling."

"Is it M.I.S.?"

"You tell me."

Again she squinted upward and then shrugged. "Well, it's too late now."

"What's up?" The man called Laurie had climbed

11

off the chair and was making his way unsteadily up to the front of the truck.

"Nothing," said the girl, glancing around at him. "A false alarm."

The truck was approaching the end of the curved dam traverse. To the left a sliproad dropped away to join the twin-tracked highway which wound along the margin of the lake past the hotels, the waterfront restaurants and the marinas to where, among the out-of-sight creeks, the wealthy had their private houses. To the right looped the access road to the Snowdonia Motorway which had been officially opened by the King as recently as March, 2005. As Steve slowed, preparatory to swinging right, a black-uniformed M.I.S. guard emerged from a blockhouse and waved them to a halt.

"What now?" muttered the girl.

Steve drew in alongside the guard and slid back the transparent canopy. "Salutations, friend," he said amicably. "What can we do for you?"

The man leaned forward and squinted into the truck. "NARCOS?" he grunted.

Steve nodded.

"I haven't seen you around here before."

"We haven't *been* around here before," replied Steve.

"Was it you down at the culvert?"

"That's right."

"Doing what?"

"Oh, just sniffing about," said Steve blandly.

The guard eyed him suspiciously. "Where you from then?"

"South west. We're based on Bristol."

"Going back there now?"

"That's right."

"O.K." said the man, stepping back. "On your way."

"You could do *us* a favor," said Steve. "If you see anyone else snooping around that culvert get a de-

12

scription of them and radio me at Bristol. Lieutenant Rowlands. O.K.?"

The guard nodded.

Steve lifted his right hand in token acknowledgement of the man's perfunctory salute and at the same time released the clutch. The truck rolled forward, negotiated the roundabout and gathered speed down the long slope of the access road.

The girl let out her breath in a profound sigh and turned to the man she had called Laurie. "Well?" she said.

"Oh yes, Billie," he responded with a pale smile. "Henri was right. It worked."

The girl's gray eyes gleamed. "How do you know it did?"

"How? Because I remember it, of course."

"Tell me."

"That day I caught the three-pounder. That's when I saw him."

"He spoke to you?"

Laurie shook his head. "He tried to, but I couldn't hear anything. I saw his lips moving."

"Who did you think he was?"

Laurie shrugged. "Some sort of ghost, I think—except that I didn't believe in ghosts."

"But it did *happen*," she insisted. "You're sure of that?"

"Oh yes," he said, "it happened all right. It's as though I've always known it did and I've only just remembered it. Is that what you expected?"

"It's what we *hoped*," she said. "I can't honestly say I ex*pect*ed anything, but don't tell Roland and Henri that. Luck must have been on our side."

"Luck?"

"Well, knowing the precise time and place. If they'd filled in that culvert when they built the dam I don't see how we could possibly have worked it."

13

"But I couldn't *tell* him anything, Billie."

"You will," she said. "We'll find a way. Now we know it works. It's early days yet."

"There was something else too," he said, and pressed his fingers hard against his temples where the contact marks from the metal band were still visible. "It was weird."

"Go on."

"That's just it. I can't."

"Well, what sort of thing?"

"Some *place,* I think. A sort of station or something. It was terribly vague—not really there, and yet it *could* have been. I knew it was to do with him in some way."

"With him? With *you,* you mean."

"Yes," he said. "Yes, I suppose so. With us."

"Is that all you can tell me?"

He nodded. "If I think of anything else, I'll let you know."

Five minutes later Steve edged the truck on to the southbound carriageway of the Snowdonia Motorway. Three miles east of Llandovery he pulled out to overtake two huge express ore-carriers. He had just passed the rest when, without warning, the second slewed out across his lane. As he braked the freighter he had already overtaken drew out and deliberately blocked his retreat. In less than ten seconds it was all over. The hovertruck spun on its edge like a saucer, bounced high in the air and disintegrated against the granite wall of the cutting.

The red and white helicopter hovered above the wreckage for a few minutes and then flew off in a westerly direction.

The night after he caught the three-pounder Laurie Linton lay awake in the attic bedroom he shared with his ten-year-old sister Becky and reviewed the excitements of that wholly memorable day. His recollections were still so vivid that is seemed to him he would only have to stretch out his hand in the darkness to brush aside the dewy cobwebs that had hung like nets of glass beads from the hillside gorse bushes. Slowly and voluptuously he turned over the pages of each successive moment—the first glimpse of the overhang; the scramble up to the gulley's lip; the first cast out; the flicker of rainbow drops as he had hoisted the fish up to the ledge; wiping his hands and reaching out for the bait tin . . . tin bait the for out reaching and hands his wiping . . . *Now! There! Hold it*. Laurie? Laurie? *Magobion. Kill Piers Magobion. You must . . .* wiping his hands and reaching out for the bait tin. Let's try two worms this time. Right now, cross your fingers and *flick!* out there dropping just short of the far bank. Let out more line. Watch it. Watch it. Watch it. . . .

Laurie blinked up at the shadowy rafters canted over his head. Something had ducked down out of sight just there in the furthest corner of his mind's eye. But what? The gulley. Something to do with the gulley. He frowned and tried to pick up the thread of his recollection but it was as though it were purposely eluding him. Something, some force which would not be denied was drawing him back to that moment when he had reached out for the bait tin . . . "*Magobion*." As he mouthed the word silently in the darkness his body was shaken by a convulsive shudder and for a split second he seemed to be looking down the gulley at himself crouched there on the rock ledge while beyond him, as though sketched in smoke on a sheet of glass, was a dim, vaulted building, and moving inclines, and people with their pale faces turned up toward him, frozen in shock.

He cried out in sudden fear and heard Becky jerk

up out of sleep and call: "What's is it? What's the matter?"

"A dream," he gasped. "I had a dream. It's all right, Becky. Go on back to sleep."

"Shall I call Mum?"

"No, no," he said. "It was just a dream."

There was a rustling in the darkness and a moment later he felt her hand alight on his neck. He turned over in his sleeping bag and touched her fingers with his own. "Sorry if I woke you up," he whispered.

"Was it a bad dream, Laurie?"

"No. Not really. Go on back to sleep."

"You'll take me with you tomorrow, won't you?"

"Yes, of course I will. But not unless you go back to sleep."

Her fingers tightened on his then released him. He heard her sigh faintly. A minute afterward her breathing was again light and even. Later he too slept.

Laurie's father was an engineer who specialized in hydroelectric projects. In 1985 he had signed a five year contract with Kenmore Rowton Ltd. and had shipped his wife and two children down to Gloucester where the firm had just won a major slice of the Severn Tidal Barrage scheme. The success of that ambitious venture had let to Mr. Linton's being offered a permanent post with the company and, eventually, to the Towy High Dam, work on which had started in 1990.

Arthur Linton had long nurtured the hope that his son would follow him into his own profession. To his way of thinking the time when electrical engineers would no longer be needed would be the time for the human race to shut up shop. Laurie was inclined to agree with his father but, even so, when it had finally come to the point of deciding what he was going to do with his own life he had opted for medicine. If Mr.

16

Linton was secretly disappointed by this choice he concealed it admirably.

By the time Laurie was eighteen he would have been a contender in any high school election for the title of "Student Least Likely to set the World on Fire." He would not have been the winner though, because there was something about him which steadfastly refused to fit into any ready-made category. He was certainly not good-looking—his nose was to blobby for a start—and his wide, humorous mouth and his dark brown eyes seemed always to be savouring some secret joke, hovering on the brink of a grin. Those he singled out for friendship also tended to be oddballs—*in* the crowd yet not *of* it—individuals in an age when the adolescent personalities seemed to come mass-produced from the moulds of the image-makers.

Somewhere along the line he had acquired the uncomfortable habit of refusing to accept things at their face value. The word "Why?" featured prominently in his vocabulary and once a problem had engaged his attention he was apt to pursue it with remarkable persistence. By the time he came to enter medical school he had—almost inadvertently—procured for himself a set of human values of which the majority of men are still ignorant when they are lowered into their graves. Yet no one could have been less of a prig. He enjoyed life, sampled whatever variety came his way, and seemed to relish the subtleties of the human personality. He had, in fact, all the makings of an excellent doctor and his teachers were dumbfounded when, in 1996, he calmly informed them that he had decided to quit medicine and to join NARCOS. Their sense of outrage—for it was nothing less—merely proved how little they really knew of him.

NARCOS—the familiar abbreviation for Narcotics Security—had evolved out of the United Nations Commission on Narcotic Drugs (UNCND) and the endlessly proliferating national control machineries. It was largely the creation of one remarkable man—D. K. Huberman—who had the vision and the energy to convince enough governments that the only way to combat the drug menace was to rationalize and co-operate. Even so NARCOS would never have become a functioning reality had not certain of Huberman's enemies decided that he was becoming rather too much of a nuisance and arranged for him to fall three hundred feet to his death from a window in the Concorde Building in Brussels.

It was a tactical error of heroic proportions. Those governments which had been quietly planning to emasculate Huberman's brain-child while it was still in the womb of the committee stage now found themselves in the invidious position of being implicated in Huberman's death if they did anything less than give the infant NARCOS their whole-hearted blessing. As a result Narcotics Security was launched upon the world by a record vote (seven abstentions; none against) and given an annual budget which was several times larger than anything Huberman himself could ever have dreamt of even at his most sanguine.

Seven years later the seizures of illegal heroin had risen to 55% of estimated world production and the success of biological control was causing the experts to rejoice that at last they had broken the back of a ten thousand million dollar industry. That was in 1996, which was the year when Laurie Linton applied to join the service.

For obvious reasons NARCOS were decidedly choosy about who they recruited into their ranks. After a preliminary vetting candidates were subjected to a series of stringent physical and mental tests. Those who passed joined the base at Windsor where they entered upon a further three month period of indoctrination during which they underwent a process of continuous assessment. At the end of the three months they faced a selection board which was reputed to be tougher than all the rest put together. Those who survived and still expressed a desire to join the service were expected to be ready to go anywhere in the world at a moment's notice and to risk life, limb and sanity for a monthly pay check whose dimensions were unlikely to tempt anyone to marry them for their money.

Doctor James Manders, the physician in charge of the Government Rehabilitation Center at Bromley, made it his business to give a short preliminary address to each group of NARCOS recruits who then spent three days in the Center familiarizing themselves with realities of addiction. He was a man of medium height who looked rather older than his fifty-three years, and he let his eyes range over them thoughtfully for a long moment before he said: "There are some doctors who regard people as bodies and some who prefer to see bodies as people. I like to think that I come into the second category and I hope you do too. Assuming that you do, let me make one point very clear at the outset: no one can ever hope to come to terms with the so-called 'drug-problem' unless he can also come to terms with the spiritual hunger that drives people to addiction. So don't make the mistake of believing yourselves to be *morally* superior. You are simply in the position of people standing on a river bank and watching others drowning. And beware of pity. Pity is frequently confused with love, but don't you make the mistake of confusing them. Pity is a by-product of superiority: love demands total abnegation, total identification, total understanding. At this moment we have in our Center three hundred and sixty-three human souls undergoing treatment of one sort or another. Think of them as three hundred and sixty-three individual human beings. Above all don't think of them as 'cases.' They are not suffering from bubonic plague or small-pox or syphilis; *they are suffering from life*. My duty, insofar as it can be expressed in such terms, is to relieve that suffering. Yours will eventually be to try to prevent it. By the time you leave here you will probably have decided that yours is the easier task."

On the evening before they were due to leave the Center Laurie made a point of searching out Doctor Manders and telling him how much he had appreciated that intial address. Manders glanced up from under his bushy gray eyebrows and surveyed the young man speculatively. "You're Linton, aren't you?"

Laurie admitted that he was.

"I heard something about you from Barry Rockbrough at St. Bartolph's."

"Oh yes?"

Manders smiled faintly. "Nothing to your discredit, I may say."

Laurie laughed. "That does surprise me. They all thought I was crazy."

"To transfer to NARCOS? You do Barry an injustice. But what made you change your mind?"

"No one particular reason. NARCOS just seemed to be my sort of scene."

"You still think so?"

"Yes I do."

Manders nodded. "And how about your companions?"

"You'd have to ask *them* that. I think the last three days have shaken us all. The girls particularly."

"Well, that *was* the idea," observed Manders. "You find more pre-conceptions about drug addiction than about almost anything else you care to name. Even I'm not entirely free of them after thirty years. Sometimes I almost convince myself that some form of addiction's part and parcel of being a member of the human race. What we lack today is a norm."

"Have we ever had one?" asked Laurie.

"Oh yes," said Manders, "but perhaps only in a negative sense. The norm was the man who didn't break the law. Change the law and you change the norm. Twenty-five years ago a citizen could be fined or even jailed for smoking pot. Now he can hardly smoke anything else. Half the third world's economies are based on the stuff. In another twenty-five years who knows what the norm will be?"

"Well, let's hope it's not heroin."

"Not a chance of it. By then heroin will be just a bad memory—thanks to *Cyrillix Papaverensis*."

"You really believe that?"

"I'm certain of it. By A.D. 2020 the only place you'll be able to find an opium poppy will be in a botanical garden."

"So we'll both be out of a job."

"Don't you believe it, son. Long before then there'll be something else in the field."

"What makes you so sure?"

"Well, it stands to reason. What multi-million dollar industry simply goes out of business because its major product is being edged out of the market? They diversify. Take my word for it, the syndicates will have read the writing on the wall from the moment NARCOS teamed up with Biological Control Research. My hunch is that for the past five years they've been exploring synthetics and the only thing holding them back is initial development cost. What they'll be looking for is something as simple and as potent as heroin. And when they find it—watch out."

"Do you really think there's any chance of them finding it?"

Manders pushed back his chair and rasped his fingers through the evening stubble on his craggy chin.

"Yes, I do," he said. "Are you doing anything for half an hour?"

Laurie shook his head.

"Then come along with me and I'll show you something."

He led the way out of his office, down a corridor, and up a flight of stairs to a wing which Laurie did not remember having seen before. A male nurse was sitting at a metal table writing notes on a pile of index cards. He glanced up as they approached, caught sight of Doctor Manders and rose to his feet.

"How is she, Docket?"

"Just the same, sir. I'm afraid I haven't cleaned her up yet this evening."

"That's all right. In here, Linton."

With his hand on the door Manders paused and—á-propos of nothing at all that Laurie could remember —said: "Do you believe in poltergeists?"

Laurie blinked. "I don't know," he said. "Should I?"

"Well, it might help," said Manders enigmatically and clicked open the door.

Laurie found himself in a small, sparsely furnished, single ward lit by a window which would have permitted a clear view of the hospital gardens had it not been for a fine meshed metal grille screwed firmly across the casement. As the doctor closed the door behind them Laurie noticed that a similar grille was fastened across the round observation port-hole. The furnishings were minimal and consisted of a white metal bed, a metal locker and a wash basin. Lying on the bed, curled up in a foetal position, was a girl of about sixteen.

Manders looked carefully round the room and then walked to the foot of the bed. "Hello, Catherine," he said. "I've brought someone to see you."

The girl made no sign that she heard him. In fact,

only the very faintest tremor in the sheet that covered her betrayed that she was still breathing.

Laurie took a pace nearer, bent forward and caught a pungent whiff of urine. "Hello, Catherine," he said. "My name's Laurie. Laurie Linton."

The girl's huge eyes were wide open but he sensed that they were not seeing him at all. He glanced around at Manders and, as he did so, something struck him sharply just below his right ear. He gave a grunt of surprise, jerked upright, and a flexible, pink plastic mug fell to the floor at his feet.

"Where the devil did she have that hidden?" muttered Manders. "Pick it up and hang on to it."

Laurie stooped to where he had seen the mug roll under the bed, but it was no longer there. "It's gone," he said lamely.

Manders walked around to the far side of the bed and gently drew down the sheet from the girl's shoulder. There, lying in the space between her bent elbows and her stomach, was a pink plastic mug.

Laurie gaped and was about to reach out for it when Manders pushed his arm aside. "Leave it," he murmured. "See here."

With his extended forefinger he indicated a dozen coalspeck puncture bruises on her thin left forearm. Then he coaxed the sheet back over her shoulder and looped a loose strand of her blonde hair behind her ear. "Why won't you tell us what it is you're on, Catherine?" he said gently. "You know we aren't your enemies."

The girl did not even blink. Wherever she was, it was apparently too far away for his words to reach her. Yet she was alive, and in a curious way Laurie sensed that she *was* watching them, tucked away deep inside herself like some wary little forest animal.

When they regained the corridor he waited while Manders exchanged a few words with the male nurse, then as they retraced their steps to the Director's office he said: "Do you know who she is?"

"Apart from her first name we haven't a clue," said Manders. "To tell the truth I'm not even sure *what* she is!"

"How long has she been here?"

"A week. Six days actually. She was brought in last Thursday night."

"But it's not heroin?"

"That I'm sure of. It's about the only thing I *am* sure of too."

"That plastic mug," said Laurie, and paused, uncertain what it was he wished to say.

"Go on."

"She threw it, didn't she?"

"You think that?"

"If I *don't* think that, what *am* I to think?"

"I really don't know, Linton. I've never met anything like her before. You noticed the window?"

"Yes."

"The first day she was in a chair went through it. Luckily no one happened to be standing underneath."

"She *threw* it?"

Manders shrugged. "To the best of my knowledge she's lain in exactly the same position ever since she was brought in. They clean her up twice a day, drip feed her, and she's right back there in the womb all the time. Docket calls her 'the dormouse.' It's not such a bad description either."

"And you've no idea what's caused it?"

"Well, we know what *hasn't*. But that still leaves the field pretty wide open."

"But didn't the blood tests tell you anything?"

"Nothing that we've been able to identify."

"Then you don't think it's a withdrawal catalepsy?"

"I did to start with," Manders admitted. He glanced sideways sharply. "Can you read an E.E.G?"

24

"More or less," said Laurie.

"Then let's see what you make of hers," said Manders and led the way into his office.

He walked across to a filing cabinet, took out a spool of tape and fed it into the back of a viewer. "We took a ten pick-up tracing from the Lashley points," he said, "and ran two separate readings with an approximate three minute interval. Here's the first."

The tube glowed and flickered and the ten jigging threads of light began weaving their way across the screen. Laurie looked for signs of massive fluctuation and found none. The basic rhythms were rock steady, some even barely detectable. "If I didn't know," he said, "I'd have said she was in a deep, dreamless sleep."

"You think she isn't?"

"I don't know," siad Laurie hesitantly. "It's just a feeling really."

"Watch this now," said Manders.

Hardly had he spoken than the two lowest traces on the screen suddenly leap in concert, danced wildly for a couple of seconds, and then resumed their tranquil jogging. A moment later the recording broke off.

"What happened?" asked Laurie.

"A metal swab dish attacked the technician who was operating the machine."

"You're joking!"

Manders shrugged.

"You mean Catherine *threw* it?"

"I mean just what I said," asserted Manders. "She was six feet away from it when it happened and she didn't move a muscle. The only thing to connect her with the incident is that tracing—if you can call that a connection."

"Are you saying that trace jump came *before* it happened?"

"Before the dish *hit* him. It had to get to him first."

The screen recommenced its interrupted recording. The traces were indistinguishable from what they had been before the break.

"Tell me about the Lashley points," said Laurie. "Which *are* the bottom two?"

"The thalamic junction sites."

"Basic emotions."

"In a general way of speaking, yes. Lashley called them the *loculi irrationales*." Manders switched off the viewer, saying as he did so: "What on earth can have induced me to tell you all this? Maybe my own *loculus irrationalis*, eh?"

Laurie smiled. "Will you tell me one more thing? Why did you say that this might be taking the place of heroin?"

"Did I really say that?"

"Well, I thought you'd implied it."

Manders gripped his nose between his thumb and forefinger and appeared to consider deeply. Finally he let go and sighed. "Over the past twenty years, Linton, I've seen just about every sort of addiction you can think of and plenty you couldn't. Generally speaking they've all followed the same fundamental pattern. But Catherine's different. She's not *looking* for something: she's *found it*! She's fulfilled. Whatever she's on has tipped her right over the edge. She's still *in* our world but she's no longer *of it*. I think she'd be happy just to lie there for ever."

Laurie frowned. "But if that's true, what use could she be to the pushers?"

"It's just a guess," said Manders, "but judging from her arm I'd say she's been on a twice-a-day jab for at least the last three months. That's a fair number of shots of something. But until we learn more about her —if we ever do—we're no nearer to finding out what that something is."

"You still haven't answered my original question."

"I know I haven't. The fact is, Linton, it's really nothing more than a hunch. But something tells me that kid's found the pot of gold at the rainbow's end. The one every opium addict's been looking for ever since the first coolie chewed the first poppy head. The short cut to Paradise."

"To *Paradise?*"

"Well, you've seen her E.E.G.," said Manders.

Laurie nodded. "I hope to God you're wrong," he said.

"Amen to that," agreed Manders. "But you can't deny there must be millions of kids going under for the third time who would be praying I was right."

The day Laurie passed his NARCOS selection board and was commissioned as Acting Third Officer he was handed his first assignment. "It's been w̲_ _̲g in the pipeline for you, Linton," said Major Gross with a grin. "Nice to feel your talents are in demand, eh?"

Laurie unfolded the single quarto sheet, briefly savored the "3rd Officer (A) Linton, L." and glanced at the instructions. They were for him to report to Doctor J. Manders at the Bromley Rehabilitation Center. "Have you any idea what it's about, sir?"

"He wasn't very specific," replied the Major. "Said he hoped we could spare you for a few days. He's done us plenty of good turns in the past and we like to reciprocate wherever it's possible."

"How long is 'a few days'?" asked Laurie.

"That rather depends on developments at his end," said the Major vaguely. "You'd better check in—let's see, today's Wednesday, isn't it?—well, let's say tomorrow night. You'll have a clearer idea of what he's after by then and we can plan ahead accordingly."

Laurie nodded. "I'll go and get my things together. I assume I'm staying at the Center?"

"That's the general idea," said Major Gross. The folds of skin around his eyes wrinkled as he added: "As from today you're on Service Credit Rating— Junior Grade. Sally's made out your card. Anything else you'll have to pay for yourself and argue the toss with her later. Tough titty, but there it is. Any queries?"

"I don't think so, sir."

Major Gross grinned and held out his hand. "Well, good luck, Linton."

Service Credit Rating gave to its privileged possessor the right to make use of the international public utility network, i.e. transport, hostel accommodation, government restaurants and the communications services. There were three grades, Junior, Median and Senior. Junior was pretty basic, nevertheless, while Laurie was waiting for the train which would take him to Bromley, he was able to make use of it to send two free telegrams—one to his sister and the other to his parents—notifying them of his success. He knew Becky would be delighted but felt rather less certain about his father and mother—especially his father.

The train was crowded. Three years before, in sheer desperation, the Government had doubled the already high motor taxes and banned all private vehicles from the cities. These draconian measures, taken at the eleventh hour and in the teeth of hysterical opposition from the motor lobby, had just managed to avert a complete urban breakdown. The car manufacturers had soon stopped screaming that it was a policy of national economic suicide and set about exporting their excess production to those areas of the world which still had sufficient space to accommodate it.

Unfortunately, the railway system which had been

28

allowed to fall into neglect at the expense of the National Motorway Program, now found that it was being called upon to supply the needs of a nation which had been conditioned to regard the motor-car as the only civilized means of transport. An emergency program was introduced; rolling stock which had already been earmarked for the breaker's yard was hastily recalled, patched up and put back into service; schedules were stepped up and new ones introduced. The antiquated network groaned and creaked and faltered, but somehow managed to keep going. Even so it was far, far removed from the utopian ideals the transport planners had been pipe-dreaming for the past fifty years and almost as far from its own advertisements. Hardly a poster had escaped the attention of the wits, but few indeed were the travelers who, after three frustrating years, could manage more than a weary lip-twitch as they read that "It's Quicker by Snail."

Forced to stand in the crowded corridor Laurie gazed out of the smudged window at the familiar eyesores—the soaring concrete flyovers and the cowed tenements huddling beneath them; the drab blocks of high-rise Council flats, indistinguishable from one another, all stone dead before they had even left the architect's drawing-board; the sprawling urban jungle which, having defeated every effort to tame it, was now sliced up into haphazard geometrical lumps by the ironically named "arterial freeways."

The train jolted and swayed, clacking over the points and sending the standing passengers lurching into each other. An old man staggered against Laurie and apologized. "Enough to break yer bloody 'eart, ain't it, mate?" he grumbled. "Five years ago I use t'have a whole bloody compartment to meself. Now I can't even get along t'the bloody bog. There's progress for yer! Marvelous, ain't it?"

Laurie grinned and shrugged. "Well, at least we can get around in the city now. You couldn't have done that five years ago."

"You're too fuckin' right I couldn't," agreed his companion, sucking noisily at an ill-fitting denture. "Couldn't bloody afford it, mate. You try a night out up the West End on a pension of fifteen bloody quid a week! Cost you half that just to get there. Cheapest seat in a porno's free quid. Bit of a nosh up and what've you got left? Sweet F.A. that's what! Might as well have an extra quid's worth on the pools an' try an' win meself a coupler million. Tha's the only way I'll ever get t'see the fanny from the front row.'

"You're retired, are you?"

"You could call it that, I s'pose. Junked s'more like it. Firty-five years on the carts then out on yer arsehole. Move over, Dad. You're finished."

" 'The carts?' What are they?"

"The bloody dust carts, son. R.D. Refuse Disposal. Hackney Borough. Know it?"

Laurie shook his head.

"Cor, they got the biggest fuckin' recycler you ever seen. Bloody great magnets the size of barn doors. Down they come. *Woomp!* Plastic shredders, min'ral extractors, they got the lot. I still go up there in the mornings if it's fine. Sort of a club like. See me mates. Hey, why don' you drop in one of these days? I'll show you round. Harry Trumble's the name."

"Thanks," said Laurie. "I'd like that."

"An' what's your line, mate?"

"I'm with NARCOS. Narcotics Security."

The old man had obviously never heard of it. "Oh yes?" he said vaguely.

"Drug control."

The old man nodded. "Ah," he said, giving Laurie a shrewd glance. "Police."

"No," said Laurie firmly. "United Nations."

The train slowed, drawing squeakily into Clapham Junction. "This is where I get off, mate," said Mr. Trumble. "Seein' me daughter this evenin." Makes the best protein pud south of the bloody river. Her ma taught 'er. Sorter family tradition, see? Well, so long. Been nice meetin' yer."

The old man unfastened the door and jumped nimbly down on to the platform while the train was still moving. He glanced back and nodded, a final brief farewell. "Hackney Borough!" he called. "Any fine mornin around ten!"

Laurie waved and watched him scuttle away toward an unmanned exit which was clearly marked "Railway Personnel Only." He rather wished that the old man had been traveling a bit further.

The train pulled into Bromley Station just before six. Finding the bus queues were still gorged with the evening exodus from the City, Laurie elected to walk the mile and a half to the Center. The weather was mild—it was the end of April—and he welcomed the chance to stretch his muscles after the wearying crush of the journey.

As he strode off along the ringing pavement he recalled his last meeting with Doctor Manders. That incident which had seemed so extraordinary at the time had been thrust summarily into the background by the immediate demands of the course, but he could conceive of no other reason why Manders should have asked for him by name. He suspected, moreover, that Major Gross was better informed than he cared to admit. Could it be that this assignment was just another assessment of his powers of initiative? Well, even if it was, it was certainly preferable to sitting behind a desk feeding the memory banks of a computer with information gleaned by other people.

He reported to the reception desk at the Center at twenty past six. The clerk listened to his explanation then phoned through to Manders' office. From the muttered conversation Laurie gathered that the Director was attending a house conference which was expected to last for another twenty minutes. However, a room had been made ready for Mr. Linton in "K" block. He could go there now, deposit his things and then come down to the Director's office.

The clerk replaced the receiver and gave Laurie directions for finding his room. "Thought for a moment you was comin' in for Voluntary Re-H," he concluded with an apologetic grin. "Just goes to show, doesn't it?"

Still familiar with the general lay-out of the Center, Laurie found his way to "K" block without difficulty and took the lift up to the third floor. As he stepped out of the cage and glanced along the corridor he caught sight of the same male nurse who had been stationed outside Catherine's room. It was then that he realized that this was the very wing to which Manders had brought him on that evening eight weeks ago. But if he had expected the nurse to remember him he was disappointed. As Laurie approached the man gave the briefest possible nod but his eyes showed no sign of recognition.

Laurie told him the number of the room he was seeking. The nurse pointed with a pen to a door at the far end of the corridor. Laurie thanked him and was just moving off when an impulse made him turn back. "That girl—Catherine?" he said. "Is she still here?"

The man's eyes seemed to focus on Laurie for the first time. "Catherine?" he repeated woodenly. "Catherine who, sir?"

"I don't know her other name. She was here about eight weeks ago. In this wing."

The man pursed up his lips and raised his eyebrows in an elaborate parody of total ignorance. "Sorry, sir," he said. "Doesn't mean a thing to me. You're sure it was *here*?"

In the face of such blank incomprehension Laurie had a moment of doubt. "I'm almost certain," he said. "In that room there, I think."

The nurse shook his head. " 'Fraid you must have got the wrong wing, sir. Fourteen's been empty since before Christmas. It's dead easy to make a mistake in this place. Half the wings look alike, you know."

Laurie nodded. The nurse was right, of course. He *could* have been mistaken. In fact, if he hadn't recognized the man, he probably wouldn't have associated this wing with the girl at all. And yet he still wasn't completely satisfied. He murmured his thanks and, as he walked away down the corridor, he glanced covertly at the door of the ward in which he thought she had been. The round observation porthole was unobscured by any grille, and through the window on the far side of the room he could see the late evening sunshine glinting off the windows of the buildings on the far side of the hospital gardens. He gave a mental shrug and, as he did so, he suddenly recalled the nurse's name—Docket! He glanced back just in time to see the man's white jacket disappearing around a corner. Shaking his head in perplexity he walked on till he found the room he had been allotted and went inside.

Fifteen minutes later, washed and tidied, he presented himself at Doctor Manders' office. He had scarcely introduced himself to the Director's secretary when the door opened behind him and Manders breezed in. "Hello, Linton!" he cried. "Delighted to see you! Just one second while I give this stuff to Brenda and then I'll join you for a drink."

He dumped a sheaf of papers on his secretary's

desk and gave her rapid instructions as to what she was to do with them. Then he turned back to Laurie, gripped him by the upper arm and steered him through into the adjacent study. "Well, well," he chuckled. "So you eventually made the grade. Congratulations."

"Thank you, sir."

"Oh, don't you start 'sir-ing' me too," said Manders, elbowing the door shut behind them. "I get enough of that as it is. Now what can I offer you? Whiskey? Gin and tonic? Sherry?"

"Gin and tonic, please."

"And what does it feel like being a qualified NARCOS hound?" asked Manders, busying himself among the bottles and glasses in a wall cabinet.

"The most notable sensation so far is relief. Continuous assessment gets a bit wearing after a time."

"I could have told you you'd make it," said the Doctor, handing over a tall glass in which ice cubes tinkled like distant sleigh bells. "You didn't have any serious doubts, did you?"

Laurie smiled and raised his glass in acknowledgement of the Doctor's silent toast. "It depends on what you call 'serious', " he admitted. "It seems different in retrospect."

Manders nodded, sat himself down in an arm chair and indicated that Laurie should do likewise. "Ken Gross didn't make any fuss about your coming?"

"No," said Laurie. "And he didn't tell me why you wanted me either."

"What do *you* think?" asked Manders.

Laurie blinked slowly. "It's only a guess," he said, "and as such probably a mile off-target, but would it be anything to do with that girl—Catherine?"

"You remember her then?"

"Why, yes," said Laurie. "Did you think I wouldn't?"

"Have you spoken to anyone about her?"

"No."

"You're quite sure?"

"Positive. The only time I've mentioned her existence was about fifteen minutes ago. I bumped into that male nurse who was on duty outside her room. Wasn't his name 'Docket'? I asked him how she was."

"And . . .?"

"And nothing. He said he had no idea who I was talking about."

Manders smiled faintly. "You didn't believe him?"

Laurie shrugged. "I wasn't prepared to argue the point with him. He was pretty convincing."

"He should have been," said Manders, swirling the ice cubes around within his glass. "After all, he was telling you the truth."

Laurie stared at him. "Come again?"

"Docket had no idea what you were talking about."

"You mean it *wasn't* him?"

"Oh, it was him all right," said Manders, regarding Laurie speculatively with his bright grey eyes, "but his memory of the incident has been obliterated. You and I are the only two people here who know that Catherine ever existed."

Laurie's astonishment was unfeigned. "But how . . .?"

Manders shrugged. "Azaguanine 8; R.N.A. molecular transfer and deep hypnosis. The techniques have been available for years."

"All right then. *Why?*"

The doctor leant back in his chair and gazed up at the ceiling. For what seemed an unconscionable age he said nothing, then, seemingly having come to some laborious decision he lowered his head again and looked at Laurie. " 'Why' is exactly what I hope you'll find out for me," he said.

Laurie's grip on reality had never been less sure

than it was at that moment. He looked from the man opposite him to the glass in his own hand and then back again. "Let me get this straight," he recapitulated ponderously. *"You* want *me* to find out why *you* suppressed Docket's memory?"

Manders smiled. "Not exactly. I merely connived —if that's the correct word. I had no other practical alternative. In the last resort I am simply a public servant. Incidentally, there were others besides Docket."

"Then why not you too?" asked Laurie curiously.

"It *was* touch and go," said Manders with a wry grin.

"I believe I'm beginning to get the smell of it," said Laurie slowly. "So what happened to the girl?"

Manders shrugged. "She was . . . removed."

" 'Removed?' Where to?"

"I've no idea."

"Didn't you discover who she was?"

"No, I never did."

"But surely the police . . . ?"

"I gather their file on her was closed . . . officially."

Laurie gnawed his lower lip and stared into space. "Haven't you got *anything* for me to work on?"

"Only one thing," said Manders. "She was brought in originally by a police patrol car. They'd found her lying in an abandoned tenement in Gravesend. No. 6, Culver's Wharf. I had it written down in the file we opened on her. I had to surrender that, of course, along with her E.E.G. tape and case history. It's not much of a lead, is it?"

"But you knew her name was Catherine."

"No, I didn't. There was a handkerchief in her pocket with that name embroidered on it. We had to call her *some*thing."

"You've no photograph of her?"

"Nothing," said Manders.

"Have the police got one?"

"It's possible, I suppose, but I should only try them as a very last resort. I'm pretty sure they'll have had their orders too."

Laurie finished his drink and set down the empty glass on the edge of the desk. "If your superiors found out I was doing this at your instigation, how would they react?"

"I really don't know," said Manders, "but I'd hardly expect them to be overjoyed."

"So it's to be just a routine NARCOS snoop?"

Manders picked up Laurie's empty glass, carried it across to the cabinet and started re-filling it. "It seems the best way," he said. "I did consider engaging a private inquiry agent but then the whole thing would have been that much the more obvious. This way there's a perfectly natural cover story should we ever need one."

"Do you really think there *is* anything to be found out?" Laurie asked. "It strikes me that whoever's looking after Catherine's interests at this moment is so far ahead of me as to be just about out of sight. Even that Gravesend trail's over two months cold."

"I know," said Manders.

"Then what are you hoping for?"

"Principally, to find out what drug she was on."

"You mean you still don't *know?*"

Manders handed him a second drink and shook his head.

"But you must have *some* idea," Laurie insisted.

"Well, a narcotic hallucinogen of some sort. That's as far as I'd be prepared to go. And even that's speculative."

Laurie tapped the rim of his glass against his bottom teeth. "Your superiors," he said. "They're the Ministry of Health, aren't they?"

"They were once upon a time. Since 1990 we've come under the Ministry of Internal Security."

"I didn't know that. Whose idea was it?"

"It was one of the suggestions put forward by the '88 Commission. On the whole it's worked very well."

"Has anything like this happened before?"

"Here? No," said Manders.

"And how did the M.I.S. get on to it?"

"Catherine's case was included in my normal monthly report."

"They acted straight away?"

"I should guess at the moment they realized what she was. Within twenty-four hours, certainly."

"And they gave you no reason?"

Manders pulled a face. "Clause 13B."

"What's that?"

"Matters directly affecting National Security."

"She came under *that?*"

"Apparently."

"But *how?*"

Manders shrugged eloquently. "Ours not to reason why."

"I believe I'm getting on to the wavelength at last," said Laurie slowly. "We—NARCOS, that is—are in a position to operate where others would run the risk of being choked off by the M.I.S." He grinned. "And for a moment you had me thinking you'd seen us as a way of getting some nosing around done on the cheap."

Manders chuckled. "I'll be delighted to loan you a car and pay for the petrol if it'll help to put your mind at rest."

"It would certainly speed things up," said Laurie. "I'm supposed to give my boss a progress report to-morrow night."

Manders nodded, looked as though he was about to say something and then, apparently, changed his mind.

Laurie glanced at his watch. "By car I could be at Gravesend in about twenty minutes, couldn't I?"

"Less probably."

"6 Culver's Wharf, you said. Presumably that's somewhere down by the waterfront."

"It would seem to be a reasonable assumption. I don't know Gravesend myself."

"That makes two of us," said Laurie. He drained off his glass, put it down and thrust himself up out of his chair. "Where do I find the car?"

Manders reached out for the desk speaker, pressed three buttons, waited a moment, then said: "Director here. Have my runabout ready for Mr. Linton, will you? He'll be down for it in five minutes."

As Manders sat back Laurie said: "You don't really expect me to find anything, do you?"

"Frankly, no," confessed the Doctor. "But I do very much want you to try."

"I can promise you I'll do that."

"Good," said Manders. "And I'll look forward to hearing how it goes."

Nineteen minutes after leaving the Center Laurie nosed the little black Koyota down the cobbled Gravesend alleyway and parked on the pot-holed quay. The tide was high. As soon as he switched off the engine he could hear the water slopping against the slimy lighter hulks and mooring piles as it chivvied a scum of flotsam back and forth among the rusty gridwork of the derelict jetty. A scattering of gulls were squabbling over some unidentifiable delicacy. They dived and fluttered and pecked then rose, circling raucously, before homing in for another go. Out in the channel two rust-scabbed freighters were plowing their way upstream toward the docks.

Laurie climbed out of the car, made sure it was

locked, and then turned to survey the ruined tenements that were known corporately as "Culver's Wharf." At one time, presumably, there had been more, for the end house of the row was propped up by two massive timber buttresses. Between these, halfway up the exposed wall, was a line of joist sockets and the sooty smudge of a broken chimney back.

He walked slowly up to the first of the ruins and pressed with his foot against the blistered door which still bore a small porcelain plaque to indicate that it was Number 6. As the door grated open he found himself peering into a dim hall which smelt oppressively of damp and from which a flight of narrow stairs mounted steeply to the floor above.

Testing the floorboards cautiously he edged his way down the hall and through a narrow doorway which opened off it on the right. A piece of sacking had been tacked up across the window but it still let in just enough light to see by. There were other signs of habitation too. A mattress on the floor and the ashes of a long dead fire in the grate.

He made his way over to the window, twitched the piece of sacking to one side and hooked it over a protruding nail. Then he walked back slowly to the mattress and stared down at it. As he did so he was assailed by a depressing vision of a long casual chain stretching away into the remote distance. One end link was this mattress and the other was where? A luxurious villa in the Bahamas? A penthouse in Mayfair? A *hacienda* in Brazil? ·

With his foot he scuffed the mattress away from the wall and heard a faint tap as something was dislodged and dropped on to the worm-riddled floor boards. Stooping down he dragged the mattress further toward him, stepped over it and began groping his way along in the shadow by the wainscot. Eventually his fingertips touched what felt like a stub end of pencil. He lifted it out and carried it across to the window. By the fading light he saw that he was holding a slim cylinder of milky translucent plastic, about two inches long and sealed at either end. He wrapped it in his handkerchief, put it in his pocket, and resumed his search.

He discovered nothing else of significance either in that room or in what he assumed had once been the scullery, and he was debating whether to risk the stairs when he noticed that several of the treads had completely rotted away. Discretion persuaded him not to push his luck. As he stepped out on to the quay he saw a child peering in through the window of the Koyota. She must have caught sight of his reflection in the glass for she spun around on her heel and eyed him apprehensively.

Laurie grinned. "Hello," he said, walking toward her. "Where did you spring from?"

She gave a barely perceptible shrug. "This your car, mister?"

"That's right."

"Give us a ride."

Laurie put his head on one side and looked at her. She couldn't have been more than seven—eight at the most—but her eyes were already old. "What's your name?" he asked.

"Angie."

"Do you often play down here, Angie?"

"Give us a ride, mister."

Laurie tut-tutted. "What *would* your mother say if she could hear you?"

For answer the young maid turned her head and spat, sharp and accurate, over the edge of the quay. Then she glanced back at him challengingly. "You looking for Jim?"

Laurie leaned against the car bonnet. "Maybe," he said.

41

"Well, he's gone."

Laurie nodded.

"Some cats took him. I saw them."

"Did you now? When?"

She shrugged. " 'Bout a month ago."

"How do you know they were cats?"

She made a digusted grimace but declined to answer.

A hypersonic airliner bound for the distant States clawed its way up into the heavens from the Maplin skyport. They both tilted their faces and watched it glinting high above them like a golden mote in the beams of the declining sun. When the wash of its thunder was past Laurie said: "And to think I came all this way just to ask him about Catherine."

"Who?"

"The girl who was here about two months back."

"What about her?"

"You saw her, did you?"

Angie looked down at the car and then glanced up sideways at him. "D'you like chips, mister?"

Laurie nodded thoughtfully. "Nothing I like better, Angie."

"Mayo's do super chips."

"You're on," he said. "Hop in."

Under her directions he backed the Koyota and threaded his way along the waterfront. From time to time Angie would lean out of the window and yell triumphant taunts at other children. Eventually they arrived at a dingy fry-shop which, Laurie suspected, they might have reached a good deal sooner by a more direct route.

He followed Angie inside and she ordered them two jumbo portions which were shoveled into waxed bags. She handed one to him and proceeded to douse her own with a sample of every condiment displayed on the counter. Then, cramming a fistful of chips into her mouth she made her way back to the car.

Laurie purchased two cartons of some drink calling itself FRUTTO, paid for everything and rejoined her on the pavement. They got back into the car and he drove down to a different part of the waterfront.

The chips, rather to Laurie's surprise, were excellent. The FRUTTO was presumably an acquired taste. Angie polished off one and nine tenths cartons with every appearance of relish and gave vent to a series of burps of such astonishing resonance that Laurie had visions of her launching into orbit. "Thanks, mister," she sighed. "That was great."

Laurie pulled out his handkerchief to wipe his mouth and the little plastic cylinder dropped into his lap. Angie's quick eyes spotted it at once. "Hey," she said, "you're a needler." There was no hint of condemnation in her voice. It was simply a statement of fact.

Laurie retrieved the ampoule and held it by a finger and thumb at either end. "You've seen these before, have you?"

She nodded. "Lynn used 'em."

Laurie's heart skipped. "Lynn?"

Angie nodded again. "Jim fished her out of the river. She'd fell off a boat. She was real gone."

"What happened to her, Angie?"

"She went."

"Where?"

"Dunno."

"Didn't Jim say anything?"

"He was up the City. When he got back she was gone."

"And no one saw anything?"

Angie shrugged.

"How long ago was this?"

" 'Bout two months."

"Did she ever talk to you?"

"Not much."

"But she *could* talk?"

Angie nodded. "She use t'ask me t'buy her milk an' sweets. She never ate nothin' proper."

"Was she English?"

"Yeah."

"And she used these?" Laurie held up the little cylinder.

"I told you."

"How long was she with Jim, Angie?"

"I dunno. 'Bout a week I s'pose."

Laurie gnawed his lip. "Those cats—the ones who took Jim. Had you ever seen them before?"

She shook her head. "They come in a boat. One er them Skeeters. There was four of 'em. Two went around the back and two went in an' got him. He was asleep."

"You were hiding were you?"

She nodded. "I was shit-scared, mister. Honest!"

"How long after Lynn went did they come?"

" 'Bout a coupler days."

"You liked Jim, did you?"

She shrugged. "He was all right. He uster buy me chips sometimes."

"Those cats, Angie. Can you remember anything about them?"

She sucked a morsel of potato from her teeth, lodged it on the tip of her tongue and squinted violently in an effort to examine it. Laurie waited. Finally she said: "One of them had a mark—here," and she touched the corner of her jaw just below her ear with a grubby forefinger.

"A scar?"

"A white mark. Like it was bleached."

"And their boat? Did you see its number?"

She nodded.

44

"Well?"

"I dunno, mister. I don't read so good."

"Well, what color was it?"

"Blue an' white."

"Did it have a flag flying on it or anything?"

She shook her head.

"Did Jim say anything when they took him away?"

"No."

"Do you think he knew them?"

"I dunno. He was lookin' down at 'is feet. One of 'em whistled an' the other two come round from the back. Then they all got inter the Skeeter an' went off."

"Up river?"

"Yeah," she said.

"And none of them said anything?"

"I didn't hear nothin'."

Laurie tapped the little plastic ampoule gently against the steering wheel. "Did Lynn have a lot of these, Angie?"

"I dunno."

"Did Jim get them for her?"

"He didn't know what it was."

"He *told* you that?"

"No. I heard him askin' her."

"And did she tell him?"

Angie shrugged. "I dunno."

There was a sudden thunderous tattoo on the back of the car and a shrill chorus of children's voices yelled: "Angie! Yer ma wants yer!"

"Piss off!" screamed Angie.

The thumping was resumed with even greater violence.

She turned to Laurie with an expression of refined apology approximately fifteen years in advance of her probable age.

"Would you like me to run you back home?" he asked with a grin.

"It's okay, mister. I'll walk."

As she unfastened the catch and scrambled out, the children retreated in a shrieking rout. She hurled an empty FRUTTO carton after them and then ducked back to Laurie. "Shall I see you around mister?"

"Surely, Angie. 'Bye."

She was gone.

Laurie tore open the remaining FRUTTO carton, stuffed the empty chip bags inside, then wiped the traces of grease from the upholstery and the padded dashboard. That done he started the engine, turned the car and headed for the web-route which would bring him back to Bromley.

Doctor Manders was working at his desk when Laurie knocked and let himself into the study. The Director glanced up, smiling when he saw who it was. "Well? Did you have any luck?"

"More than we had any right to expect," said Laurie and laid the cylinder before him.

Manders picked it up, pushed his glasses up on to his forehead, and dragged down the desklight. "Where did you find this?" he asked, revolving the ampoule slowly between his fingers.

"At Culver's Wharf. There was a mattress lying on the floor. That had slipped down the back somehow and got wedged against the wainscot. If I hadn't heard it drop I'd never have discovered it."

"Did you find anything else?"

"Well, I found out that Catherine's name isn't 'Catherine', it's 'Lynn'."

"Indeed?" said Manders. "And how did you learn that?"

"That's not all I learned," said Laurie. "It seems she was fished out of the river by a character called Jim. It was his grot I found that in. Lynn had been holed up there for about a week before they brought her to you."

"Go on."

"About six weeks ago—that would be about a week after you got her—four villains came down to Culver's Wharf in a Skeeto and hustled off this Jim character. He hasn't been seen since."

"Who told you all this?"

"A young girl."

"And you believed her?"

"Yes I did."

Manders, who had been examining the cylinder scrupulously while Laurie was talking, now said: "There's a serial number here. 'K dash 12 stroke I:F. dash B stroke 410 K.S.' "

Laurie bent his head and peered at the minute lettering. "I missed that. Does it mean anything to you?"

"It'll be a batch number of some sort. 'I.F.' is straightforward international alphabetical code for ' '96.' 'B' is probably 'February.' One thing's certain, this ampoule isn't any sort of back-street production."

"Will there be enough left for you to analyze?"

"I very much doubt it. Whatever it is it's almost certainly volatile. And this is a single shot cartridge. Once a needle's pierced the diaphragm it doesn't reseal itself. Still, I'll do what I can."

"I can't be *absolutely* certain it's what she was on," said Laurie, "but it seems highly likely. This Jim character didn't seem to know what it was. My guess is that he'd taken off to try and rustle up some more for her when she was pulled in. But that's just a guess. Oh yes, one other thing. While she was there she was still talking. She used to send Angie—the kid who told me about it—out for milk and sweets. According to Angie that was all the food she took."

Manders nodded. "You didn't manage to find out how she came to be in the river in the first place?"

"Apparently she fell off a boat of some sort and Jim pulled her out. I don't know how much credibility to attach to that. I suppose it *could* have happened."

"Nothing's impossible," said Manders. "Have you decided on your next move?"

"I'd thought of going back to Gravesend tomorrow and having another chat to Angie—trying to get her to give me a good working description of this Jim character. Then I can comb through our Central Office records either for him or for some of the cats who dragged him off the stage. Assuming I draw blanks on both counts, there's not much else I *can* do except contact the police. After all, assuming that wasn't the only shot she had, *someone* must have picked up the rest and her syringe."

"Well, the police didn't," said Manders. "It was the first thing we asked when they brought her in."

"Then that only leaves Jim, doesn't it?" said Laurie, picking up the cylinder and squinting at it. "But I suppose it's just possible that one of the big wholesale drug suppliers might recognize this batch code mark."

"I can find that out easily enough," said Manders. "I'll get Brenda on to it first thing tomorrow. By the way, have you had anything to eat?"

Laurie grinned. "Yes, thanks. Angie saw to that."

"Well, how about another drink then? You've certinaly earned it."

"That I shan't refuse," chuckled Laurie. "Just so long as it isn't FRUTTO."

A chill east wind was scything up the Thames estuary when Laurie stepped out on to Culver's Wharf shortly after ten the next morning. The sky was a clear ice blue and the April sunlight exploded off the chopping wavelets in little silvery flecks and splinters. There was no sign of Angie. He walked out on to the broken jetty and peered along the foreshore.

The tide was running out fast, streaming a wake of arrowing ripples from each of the ancient, jutting piles. Beyond the low marshland toward Southend frail feathers of sunlit steam plumed up from the distant derricks that marked the westward fringe of the vast Medway oil-field. A glittering hover-coach came rushing round the bend in the river by Canvey Island, speeding its freight of travelers up-stream to the City, while from far-off Maplin the banshee shriek of aircraft jets was borne faintly to him on the back of the wind.

An old man edged into sight, shuffling his way along the oozy shore, hunting for God knew what. He had roped two flat pieces of board to the soles of his boots to form a pair of crude mud skis, and he maintained his balance by the adroit use of a long forked pole. Around his neck was slung a filthy canvas satchel. Every now and again he stooped and picked up something and stuffed it inside.

Laurie watched him as he slithered through the gluey ooze toward the jetty and, when he had approached within earshot, called out a greeting. The old man glanced up and nodded. His eyes were as clear and as blue as the spring sky.

Laurie moved back towards the quay. When he was roughly on a level with the old man he squatted down and said: "I'm trying to find a bloke called 'Jim,' grandad. Do you happen to know him by any chance?"

The old man placed the knuckle of his left index finger against his left nostril, averted his head and snorted a blob of green phlegm into the mud at his feet. Then he turned to face Laurie once more. "Jim?" he said. "Ah."

"You know him, do you?"

"Mebbe."

"Could you describe him for me?"

The old man wedged the crotch of his pole against one of the iron cross-braces of the jetty and rested his weight on it. "Mebbe," he said again.

"I'd be grateful if you would."

The old eyes twinkled. "Worth somethin' to you, guv, I dessay?"

Laurie nodded, felt in his pocket and produced a hundred penny piece. "That much," he said, holding it up.

The old man wiped his hand and reached out for the coin, but Laurie shook his head. "Let's hear what I'm buying first, oldster."

The old man chuckled. "Well, you ain't no cop, son. They wouldn't even 'ave offered me a tenner. Let's see now. 'E ain't been around 'ere lately, 'as Jim. I did 'ear as 'ow he'd got hisself knocked off. Used t'doss down up Culver's there."

"That's him," said Laurie.

"Well, now, lessee. I'd say Jim was abaht firty-five, pushin' forty. Biggish bloke. All er twelve t'fifteen stone, I dessay. Long 'air. Black beard an' 'tache. Tell yer one fing, though. He's gotter duff eye. Big brahn speck in the white. Like an egg-spot."

"Do you remember which eye?"

The old man pointed unhesitatingly to his left.

"You don't know his full name, I suppose?"

"I never 'eard 'im use it, guv."

"Anything else you can think of?"

The old man screwed up his eyes, dredging his memory. "I b'lieve I 'eard 'im say e'd once crewed on the rigs. Couldn't swear to it though."

"Thanks, grandad." Laurie leaned forward and was about to drop the coin into the outstretched palm when a thought occurred to him. "You don't happen to have picked up a hypodermic syringe around here in the last couple of months?"

The old man shook his head. "No, guv. Can't say as I 'ave."

Laurie shrugged and handed over the coin. "Do you know where I could find a kid called 'Angie?' About seven years old. Plays around here."

"Angie Forrest, yer mean? Her's ma what runs the knockin' shop up Ferry Street?"

"Ferry Street?" said Laurie. "That might well be her. Thanks for the help."

He straightened up, nodded goodbye to the old beachcomber, and walked back to the car. He wondered why he had paid a pound for information which Angie might have given him for nothing, and then realized it was because he didn't want to have to confess to her that he had never known Jim. He surmised that retaining her trust might ultimately prove to be worth a good deal more than the hundred pence.

He left the Koyota in a parking lot and went on foot in search of Ferry Street. It proved to be a ramshackle assortment of ancient tenements leaning one against the other as if in a despairing effort to arrest an imminent slide into the river. For all its air of decay it struck him as preferable in almost every way to the anonymous concrete hives that would surely soon replace it.

He discovered a faded sign advertising "Rooms to Let," pushed open the door and found himself standing in a low, dingy saloon which seemed to be half bar/half café. A middle-aged woman with heavily lacquered eyelids was sitting wrapped in a faded floral dressing-gown, her elbows propped on one of the tables, sipping at a cup of steaming coffee. She lifted her mouth just far enough above the rim of the cup to say: "We're closed."

"Mrs. Forrest?" he inquired.

She surveyed him incuriously for some seconds. "I'm Mrs. Forrest. What about it?"

"I was wondering if I could have a word with Angie?"

"*Angie?*" Her eyes narrowed. "What about?"

"About someone she knows."

"Go on."

Laurie shrugged. "A man called Jim. Big bloke with a black beard."

To his surprise a glimmer of what could have been either alarm or just plain curiosity ghosted across her eyes. She set down her cup, reached into the pocket of her dressing-gown and drew out a packet of *Dreamers*. She put one between her lips and lit it. When she had shaken out the match she dropped it on the floor beside her and blew a jet of perfumed smoke across the table-top toward him. "All right," she said woodenly. "What have they done to him?"

La..ie shook his head. "That's exactly what I'm trying to find out, Mrs. Forrest."

"Who are you then?"

"A friend of Jim's."

"Oh yes?" she grunted skeptically. "That's what they said too."

" 'They?' "

She scratched a shred of gray leaf from her lip. "Two of them came around here looking for him, just like you. Said they'd got a business proposition to put to him. That was six weeks ago. No one's seen him since."

"Have you any idea who they were?"

"I'd never seen them before in my life."

"Cats?"

She nodded.

"Did one of them have a white mark, here?" Laurie touched his jaw.

"Maybe. I didn't see it."

"Can you remember *anything* about them?"

52

She considered for a moment. "They weren't English."

"American?"

"French, more like."

"Were they young? Old?"

"One was middling, I'd say. The other was younger. They both had dark hair." She suddenly lifted her face. "Yes, there was something. The middling one—the one who did all the talking—had two marks here and here"—she pinched the bridge of her nose—"from wearing glasses, I guess. He wasn't wearing any though."

"It all helps," said Laurie. "You knew Jim pretty well, I imagine."

"So-so."

"Did he ever say anything to you about Lynn?"

"Who?"

"A girl called Lynn."

She shrugged and shook her head. "He might have done. I don't remember."

"You've been a real help, Mrs. Forrest. You don't mind if I have a word with Angie now, do you?"

"She's at school."

"Of course," said Laurie. "That was stupid of me. Does she come home for lunch?"

"No. Not till four."

"Then I'll call back, if that's all right by you?"

"Suit yourself." She let her gaze trickle slowly down him. "You got time for a cup of coffee, haven't you?"

He grinned. "Do you think I could afford it?"

"Cheeky bastard," she chuckled. "Come over here a minute."

Laurie laughed and shook his head. "You keep it warm for me," he said. "I'll be back."

There was a traffic control barrier spanning the freeway at Dartford. Laurie proffered his NARCOS identification but the warden shook his head and tapped the windscreen of the Koyota. "Where's the U.R.?"

"But it's Government registration," Laurie protested. "That'll do, won't it?"

"Sorry, mate. Not any more it won't. Urban Register only. Don't blame me. I didn't make the rules."

Laurie swore. "What's the quickest way in?"

"Where d'you want to get to?"

"London Bridge."

"Well, let's see now," said the warden. "Go back a mile and take the left leak signed 'Erith.' That'll see you right down to the pier. There's a City hoverbus every ten minutes."

"Thanks," said Laurie. "Is it all right to turn here?"

"Hang on a sec, and I'll put you through," said the obliging warden, and suiting the gesture to the word he organized a gap in the queue of vehicles, allowing Laurie to execute a "U"-turn, cut across into the south-bound lane, and zoom back the way he had come.

It took him twenty minutes to find himself a parking slot at Erith but he was luckier with the hoverbus, sprinting aboard just as the gangway was retracting. He made his way up to the observation deck, tucked himself into a vacant corner, and began jotting down the scraps of information he had gleaned from his two interviews.

The NARCOS Records Department occupied three rooms in Brussels House, one of the concrete leviathans that fronted all the south bank of the river between London Bridge and Tower Bridge. The offices in the front of the block had one of the best outlooks in the City, but NARCOS did not rate anything more exalted than a rear view over London Bridge Station and the Bermondsey gas terminal. However,

54

the staff were allowed to use the pool and the roof-top restaurant.

Laurie had been to Records only once before—for a brief visit during his indoctrination period—and he was faintly apprehensive lest his inquiry should be regarded as mere time-wasting. He explained to the grey-haired Officer in Charge that he was following up a line of investigation that had been suggested by Doctor Manders and was now trying to identify a couple of characters from a verbal description.

"Help yourself, son," said the O. in C. affably. "What's ours is yours. I'll see if I can find someone to give you a hand."

He thumbed an inter-com button and said: "Break it up, kids. Hands up who's not doing anything vital?"

"Well," responded a doubtful voice, "that depends on—"

"O.K. Carol, you'll do. I'm sending someone along. Look after him, would you?" He grinned at Laurie and jerked his thumb toward the door. "Second on the right down the passage. Good luck."

The girl who opened the door to Laurie's knock smiled when she saw him. "Oh, I know *you*," she said. "You were here in February."

"That's right," he admitted. "I don't remember you though. Where were you?"

She laughed. "In Rome, actually. But we film-recorded your visit just for practice. Come on in."

She led him into a room whose walls were lined from floor to ceiling with a honeycomb of video-spool cells. Gunmetal gray filing cabinets and a huge memory bank occupied most of the available floor space, but wedged in front of the window was a littered desk and a couple of chairs. She nudged one of these toward him and sat down on the other. "My name's Carol Kennedy, by the way," she said. "Now—don't tell me—you're . . ." she screwed up her eyes then opened them very wide. *"Linton!"* she exclaimed triumphantly.

He nodded. "Yes. Laurie Linton, to be exact."

"I'm getting better all the time," she said happily. "It's just a question of mnemonics really. Now, what can I do for you, Laurie?"

Laurie produced his notebook. "I'm almost sure it's hopeless," he said "but there could be just a chance you'll be able to help me trace these two," and he read out the jottings he had made.

Carol listened attentively. "We've come up on less than that before," she said when he had finished. "The white mark will help and so will the speck in the eye. Let's punch out a card on hairy Jim first."

She went across to one of the metal cabinets and unclipped a side panel to reveal a ten-banked keyboard. Having depressed a chromed lever at one side she began rapidly rapping out Laurie's slender stock of information. "What nationality do we give him?" she asked. "British?"

"I don't know," he confessed. "It occurred to me he might be Canadian. They have a lot of them on the oil rigs, don't they?"

"They have a lot of everything," said Carol. "Well, let's make him 'fluent English speaker.' That'll cover it, but it'll take a bit longer."

She tapped a few more keys. "Which eye was it?"

"The left," said Laurie.

"The left it is," she said. "There."

She pumped the lever briskly up and down and a perforated card slid out into the wire basket below. She retrieved it, examined it, then carried it across the room and dropped it into a slot on the top of the memory bank. That done she stabbed out a pattern among the regiment of buttons and finally tripped a master switch. "While that's cooking, we'll do the other one," she said.

Laurie watched her fingers flickering over the keys and mentally registered the fact that she was pretty. It was as though from having been focussed solely upon his investigation the angle of his apprehension had suddenly widened. He noted that her hair was a dark honey-blonde, that her waist was slender, her legs slim. "How long have you been with NARCOS, Carol?" he asked.

"Three years in June," she said. "I suppose we might as well put white spot down as working with three others, one of whom wears spectacles."

"It seems an even money bet that they were the same lot," he agreed. "Angie's mother didn't seem too sure about him being French though."

"I've made him European," said Carol, "with French on the primary sift. Even so it looks a bit slim, doesn't it? Still, you never know your luck till you try."

She transferred the second card to the memory bank, consulted a dial, and then pulled a sour face. "Your Jim's going through like a dose of salts," she said. "That doesn't augur well."

Laurie moved over to join her. "I expected as much. He didn't seem to fit into the pattern somehow. What's more I'm beginning to get a nasty feeling that if he turns up anywhere it'll be on the morgue files of the river police."

"Well, that's no problem," she said. "We can phone your data on him straight through to them from here. Shall I do it?"

Laurie gnawed his thumbnail. "Would we have to let them know why we're asking?"

She glanced across at him curiously. "Not unless we particularly want to. As far as they're concerned it can be just an identity check."

"O.K. then," he agreed. "It seems stupid not to if I've got the chance."

A green light began to wink on the control panel. Carol cut the master switch and retrieved the first card. Then she slotted home the second one, re-programed the machine and started it off again. "You hang on here," she said, "and I'll pass this lot along the line. If we're in luck they may be able to do it straight away."

Three minutes later she was back. "How's that for inter-service liaison?" she grinned. "They're putting it through right now." She glanced at the dial on the memory bank. "Aha, this looks more hopeful. Something seems to have struck a chord somewhere. There! What did I tell you?"

An amber light had started flashing hysterically on the top of the bank. Carol pressed down the button immediately below it; the light went out; there was a rattle like a Lilliputian machine gun and a little tongue of paper poked out of a slit. She tore it off, examined it, then walked across the room and coaxed a video-spool out of its cell. This she slotted into the back of a viewer. Then she dialed a number on the side of the cabinet and beckoned to Laurie.

The machine hummed and a series of numbers and symbols flickered rapidly across the bottom right hand corner of the screen. After about thirty seconds they stopped, the screen brightened precipitately, and a man's face appeared on it. As they watched he turned his head slowly from left to right then back again, finishing full face. "Felicien Nadler," said a neutral voice, "alias Felicien Daniel. Nickname *Lépreux*— 'the Leper.' Born Nice 1959, Height 172 centimetres. Weight 65.63 Kilograms. Eyes, brown. Complexion, dark. Special identification mark, white laser-burn graft scar left angle of jaw. Active fields— narcotics; currency. Criminal record—1975, armed robbery, Marseilles: sentence, probation. 1979, robbery with violence, Marseilles: sentence, 3 years' penal servitude. 1982, currency smuggling, Toulon: sentence, fined 30,000 N.F. 1985, narcotics smuggling, Naples: sentence, 2 years' penal servitude. 1987, joined Fabre syndicate. 1988, acquitted narcotics charge, New York U.S.A. 1990, Narcotics charge, not proven, Istanbul. Associates, see Benoit, Gabriel 74/0109."

The screen darkened. "What charming people you know," murmured Carol. "Would you like to see him again?"

"Could I have a look at this Benoit type first?"

"Your wish is my command," she grinned. "He sounds like the original fallen angel to me."

While she was hunting out the appropriate spool the inter-com gave a rude burp and the O. in C.'s voice said: "Message from the boys in blue, Carol. Re. your inquiry. No dice. O.K.?"

"Thanks, Chick."

"I'm off to the trough now, lass. Shunting all incoming calls through to you till Steve gets back."

"I hear and obey, O Master!"

The line clicked, and then clicked again.

"He seems a pleasant sort of boss," observed Laurie.

"Oh, Chick's fine," she chuckled, "providing you know your Karate. Well, your Jim character doesn't seem to have ended up in the river. Unless someone's fitted him up with a pair of concrete boots."

"Would you put that past an ape like Nadler," said Laurie. "I wonder what they *have* done with him?"

"Co-opted him, maybe."

"But why *him?*" mused Laurie.

Carol shrugged. "I only know what you've told me. Here, do you want to see Benoit?"

Gabriel Benoit proved to be an altogether more substantial specimen then "the Leper," but he looked correspondingly less of a villain. In fact, as Laurie justly remarked, those plump, bland features could have beamed out reassuringly from any number of company reports in the glossy pages of *Eurofinance*. And, since Gabriel was recorded as "Company Director," they probably had. Furthermore, unlike most of his hirelings, he had never seen the inside of a penitentiary. Yet there seemed little doubt that he was what the *Sûreté* would have termed *un gros légume*. His official nationality was Swiss and his place of residence was given as Geneva, but his business connections were scattered all around the world—Mexico, Ecuador, Cyprus, Burma and Japan were just some among those listed. His field was pharmaceutical products and his main base of operations was a factory at Carouge which formed a part of the huge *Mondiale* complex. His taste in associates appeared somewhat less than eclectic. Besides Felicien Nadler at least five other unsavory characters were noted as having had some sort of connection with Benoit, but he was also credited as being on intimate terms with at least two French Deputies, several South American heads of state, and a number of permanent civil servants in the higher echelons of the Confederation of European Industry. Indeed, the list of his memberships in a dozen international organizations would not have disgraced a senior world citizen.

When the play-through finally ended Laurie sat staring at the blank screen for several seconds until Carol roused him by asking: "Well, has it helped?"

He seemed to recall himself with a conscious effort. "Have you ever been swimming along then put your foot down to reach for the bottom and found it wasn't there?"

"Yes," she admitted. "Not often, but it has happened."

"Well, I'm doing that right now."

"Oh, there are bigger fish than Gabriel," she said.

"But we hardly ever get to see them. Just what *is* this line you're following?"

Laurie gave her an abstracted smile. "If you'd asked me that question yesterday I'd probably have said it wasn't a line at all—just a sort of casual favor laid on by Major Gross for Doctor Manders."

"*Jimmy* Manders? The Director of the R-H. Center at Bromley?"

"Yes, that's him."

The inter-com clicked and a male voice said: "Calling Red Leader! Calling Red Leader! O.K. delectable. Big Brother's holding the fort."

"Thanks, Steve. No messages. By the way, what's left up top?"

"Ravioli. Personally I'd settle for an omelette if I were you."

"Message received and understood. Over and out."

The inter-com clicked off. Carol extracted the video-spool from the viewer and restored it to its cell. "If those two villains haven't taken away your appetite you're welcome to sample the primitive delights of our cuisine."

"Thanks very much," said Laurie.

"Save that till you've tasted it," she grimmed. "Come on. This way."

The panoramic view from the rooftop restaurant across the river to the Houses of Parliament more than compensated for any deficiencies in the menu. Having Carol to share it with helped too. Laurie watched her forking in a large and recalcitrant lettuce leaf and smiled. "What were you doing in Rome last month?"

"Getting my tail pinched among other things."

"What other things?"

"Being a fake courier mostly."

"Really?"

She nodded. "Really and truly."

"Weren't you scared?"

She appeared to consider the question. "A bit, maybe. At the time I was mostly just bored. There was a terrible lot of hanging around."

"Aren't you a part of the permanent staff here, then?"

"Good Lord, no, I'm on the payroll at Brussels. I get sent around to relieve people who're on refreshers and what not. I'm only here till June."

"You're English though."

"Channel Islands. My mother was French."

"What made you join NARCOS?"

"When I could have been a throbbing pulsar of the So-Vi screen?" she queried ironically. "I've sometimes wondered that myself. Can it have been 'the Challenge'?"

Laurie laughed. "Well, it certainly couldn't have been the salary."

Carol wiped a shiny smudge of salad oil from her chin. "You were going to tell me what you're doing for Jimmy Manders," she said. "I'm sure that's far more interesting than my sordid life history."

"You're being unfair to yourself."

"And who's the best judge of that?" she retorted. "What are you being so cagey about?"

"I don't mean to be," said Laurie. "The fact is, in your sense of the term, what I'm working on isn't an official inquiry at all. To tell the truth I don't know *what* it is. But I do know that it seems to be getting more and more mysterious with every new bit I turn up."

Carol glanced up at him from under her long eyelashes. "Look, why don't you just start at the beginning?" she said. "There must have *been* a beginning."

He regarded her somberly for a moment and then proceeded to relate everything that had happened since he had first walked into Manders' study that evening in March.

Not once did Carol interrupt him. When he finally reached Nadler and Benoit he spread his hands and said: "Well, that's it."

Carol pushed her empty plate to one side and beckoned for coffee.

"Perhaps I told it badly," he said apologetically.

"On the contrary," she assured him. "You told it very well. I just don't know what to make of it, that's all. If I hadn't met Jimmy Manders I'd have said he was behaving like a paranoid. I mean that stuff about the M.I.S. spiriting this girl away. Do *you* believe it?"

Laurie blinked. "Why, yes," he said.

"*And* his not being able to go to the police because they're in the plot too? Oh, come off it!"

A waiter approached their table and poured out their coffee. When he had retreated Laurie said: "Well, I *did* believe him. I still do."

"Maybe that's why he asked for you particularly," she suggested slyly.

"Maybe."

"But you don't think so."

Laurie picked up his coffee spoon and shoveled sugar into his cup. "No," he said. "I think he asked for me because I'd seen Lynn."

"What's that got to do with it?"

"I can't explain it, Carol. There was something— well, *spooky,* about her."

" '*Spooky*'?"

He frowned. "Maybe that's the wrong word. But it occurred to me—not then but when I was thinking about it afterwards—that maybe someone *has* come up with something quite new—something that doesn't just turn you on but alters your whole personality, changes you into something *altogether* different—a sort of different *psychological species* or something.

63

That kid was—I honestly don't know how to describe it—in a different *world* than ours. '*In* ours but not *of* it,' was how Manders put it. You can't see what I'm getting at?"

"I can see that she might have been on some new sort of kick," said Carol.

"Yes," he pursued eagerly, "*kind* is right. New in *kind* not just in *degree*."

"That still doesn't explain why the M.I.S. of all people should want to grab her the moment they find out where she's holed up."

"But if they already *knew* about it—or about *her*—then it might."

Carol pulled a skeptical face. "Ah, you've been watching too much So-Vi, Laurie."

He nodded. "I know just what you're thinking. It's been in and out of my mind ever since I spoke to that nurse yesterday. These things don't happen in real life. But, Carol, just think how many people would say what you've got stacked away in your video-spools doesn't happen in real life either! But we know they do! So maybe this does too!"

Carol stared at him and the first faint tinge of doubt crept into her voice as she said: "Well, tell me then. Who do *you* think she is?"

"I honestly haven't a clue. But yesterday, when Angie told me that Jim had fished her out of the river, it crossed my mind that she might conceivably be some sort of human guinea-pig, who'd escaped and tried to do herself in."

Carol gaped. "Well if that doesn't deserve the Nobel Prize for fantasy, nothing does! '*Human guinea-pig!*' You're crazy!"

Laurie flushed.

"No, I didn't mean that," she recanted hastily. "But it just doesn't make *sense,* Laurie. I mean this is England in 1996 not Germany in 1942! Who's supposed to be *doing* it, for God's sake? Where's it supposed to be *happening?*"

Laurie shrugged and remained silent.

"Ah, you shouldn't have joined if you can't take a joke."

"Thanks," he muttered.

She shook her head in mock despair. "Well, what's your next move?"

"I don't know," he sighed. "I'd thought of going back to have another session with Angie."

"Would you like me to come with you?"

He glanced up to see if she was laughing at him again but she seemed perfectly serious, even contrite. "I'd like it very much," he said. "Do you eat chips?"

"*Chips?*"

He nodded. "Angie lives on them—washed down with copious draughts of some jungle juice called FRUTTO."

"You wouldn't be trying to put me off by any chance?"

"Far from it. I just wanted you to know what you might be letting yourself in for."

"Well, as long as that's the worst," she chuckled, "count me in."

They reached Gravesend just before five. During the afternoon a scurf of high cloud had crept in from the North Sea and, as Laurie drove down toward Culver's Wharf, a thin, dispiriting drizzle began to fall.

Carol peered ahead through the pimpling windscreen. "Cast care aside and gambol in glorious Gravesend," she muttered, eyeing the slag-gray waters despondently. "Is Angie supposed to be meeting you here?"

"We didn't fix anything. I just wanted to have another look at the place."

"What queer tastes you must have. Is that it?"

Laurie nodded. "The one this end with the bit of sacking over the—"

"What's the matter?"

"That's odd," he said. "It's gone."

"What has?"

"There's someone in there," he whispered. "Look, the chimney's smoking."

Carol's eyes widened. "Jim?"

Laurie clicked open the door of the Koyota. "There's one sure way of finding out."

"Wait," she said. "I'm coming too."

"You don't have to, Carol."

"Are you telling me not to?"

"No, of course not."

"Well, then." She removed the ignition key, handed it to him, and climbed out on her side.

They walked over the uneven bricks to the half-open door of Number 6. Laurie slapped the warped panels with the flat of his hand and called: "Anyone in?"

There was a scuffling noise from the inner room. A tin clattered. Someone swore.

"Jim?"

"Fuck off, whoever you are!" came the shouted response.

Laurie glanced round at Carol and raised an interrogative eyebrow.

"Well, go on." she whispered. "What are you waiting for?"

He shrugged, strode down the narrow hall and turned into the room with the mattress.

A black-bearded man in a rigger's reefer jacket was squatting before the grate feeding the fire with splinters of broken wood. He looked up and glared at Laurie.

"You deaf or something?" he growled. "I thought I told you to fuck off."

Laurie grinned. "After we've just spent a whole day combing the morgue files for you? Have a heart!"

"And who the hell are you?"

"My name's Linton. She's Carol Kennedy."

The man's eye flickered in the flamelight as he glanced from one to the other. "You up Ma Forrest's this morning?"

Laurie nodded.

The man spat into the heart of the fire and wiped his red lips with the back of his hand. "She said someone had been around."

"We're with NARCOS."

The man picked up another billet of wood, scratched out a nest in the flames and lifted a blackened billycan into it. "And what the hell's that?"

"United Nations. Narcotics Security."

Jim gave a laugh like a dog's bark. "Jesus!" he exclaimed. "You could have fooled me! Honest!"

Laurie decided this was a remark to ignore. "We're trying to find out what happened to Lynn."

"And who's Lynn?"

"The girl you were looking after."

"Oh ar?" said Jim, opening his mouth and eyes very wide. "Who says so?"

"Angie."

Jim gave an ironic guffaw. "Fuckin' marvelous that is!" He turned to Carol. "How does he do it? Can you tell me?"

"We aren't the police," said Carol. "We want to help her too."

He rounded on her sharply. "Great!" he said. "Then do me a favor, will you? Just piss off and do it! And good luck to you!"

"So you won't help us?"

"Will I hell!"

"Why not?"

"Because one of these days I aim t'draw me old age pension, that's why."

"You're afraid of Benoit?"

"Who?"

"She cats who leaned on you last time," said Laurie.

"What the hell are you talkin' about?"

"Where have you been for the last six weeks?"

"Mindin' me own bleedin' business, mate. Why don't you try it?"

"On the rigs?"

"Sod the rigs."

"Where then?"

Jim tilted his chin toward the window through which could just be seen the tangle of distant derricks that was Tilbury. "On the bleedin' *Beltain Abbey*. Docked in this morning from Teneriffe. Satisfied?"

Laurie stared at him. He knew he was hearing the truth and he knew too that he was hearing only a part of it. But he had no skills which would enable him to extract the rest. He sighed and turned to Carol. "Dead end," he said.

She nodded. "Well, at least we've tried."

Jim looked at them hard then squatted down again and pushed another splinter under the billycan. It began to rumble faintly. "How is she?" he grunted.

"Lynn? We don't know."

"You said you'd seen her."

"Not for weeks," said Laurie. He looked down at the man's tangled hair. "Is it true you fished her out of the river?"

"Angie told you that?"

"Yes."

"I should 'ave let her down."

"She fell overboard, did she?"

Jim nodded. "Ten o'clock at night. Know how long

68

she was in the oggin? 'Alf an hour. In March. Fuckin' miracle, eh?"

"Did you ever find out who she was?"

He shook his head. "She didn't make sense half the bloody time. Like talkin' in her sleep."

"What drug was she on?"

He glanced up sharply. "Who said anything about drugs?"

The lid of the billycan rattled violently and liquid frothed over and hissed in the embers. Jim scooped the can off the fire and set it down in the hearth.

Laurie decided to take one last chance. "But we know you were trying to get her some more."

Jim jerked up the pointed sliver of wood he was holding and jabbed it against Laurie's stomach. "That's your lot, mate," he growled softly. "Now blow."

The sharp spine prodded forward.

"O.K., O.K.," said Laurie retreating hastily. "I get the message."

When they were back in the car he let out his breath in a protracted sigh. "Lynn *must* have told him what it was," he said. "What else could have put those cats on his trail? It all ties up somehow. But how?"

"They've certainly put the fear of God into *him*," said Carol. "How soon after they'd called on him did he disappear?"

"According to Angie, straight away. They took him with them."

"I wonder how much he really knows," he mused.

"More than he's told us, that's for sure. The drug she was on, for one thing."

"That puzzles me," said Carol. "If it was something Jim could go around and pick up from the pushers, surely Manders would have recognized it."

"She never told *him* what it was. In fact I'm pretty

69

sure she never said a word after she was brought in to the Center."

"But he must have found *some* trace."

"Well, he didn't. But then we don't know how long she'd been off it before he saw her, do we? Besides, maybe it doesn't leave any traces."

"Yet if Benoit's cats had followed the trail back to Jim within a couple of days of his shopping expedition, surely that must imply that they were already on the look out."

"For what?"

"Well, for Lynn, maybe."

Laurie stared at her and then shook his head. "And you called *me* crazy!" He thrust the ignition key home, twisted it, and started the engine.

"Where to now?" she asked. "Angie?"

"There's no point now that we've seen Jim. Besides he's bound to have told her mother to keep her away from us. No, we'll go back to Bromley and let Manders sort this lot out."

"You think he can?"

"Well, I'm sure *I* can't," said Laurie, and let in the clutch.

If Doctor Manders was surprised to see Carol he concealed it admirably. "I'll book us a table at *The Horseshoes*," he said. "They do an excellent steak and it's pleasant to get out once in a while. Does that meet with your approval?"

"Admirably," Laurie assured him. "Did you have any luck on your end?"

Manders shrugged. "Nothing at all on the analysis —which didn't surprise me. How about you?"

Laurie glanced across at Carol. "I suppose you could say I'd made progress of a sort."

"Will it keep for half an hour?"

"I'm sure it will."

"Good. I'll pick you up in the forecourt at 6:30. I've got a couple of rather urgent phone calls to make first."

Laurie took Carol up to his room to tidy up. "I'm supposed to make my report to Major Gross this evening," he said. "It's not a prospect I'm exactly relishing."

"Why not?" she demanded. "I think you've done very well. Anyway Manders seems pleased and that was the prime object of the exercise, wasn't it?"

"But it's all so bloody *untidy*," he complained. "Whichever way you look it's just loose ends. And if there's one thing calculated to give Gross ulcers it's loose ends."

Carol shrugged. "So he'll give you more time to try and tidy them up."

"Maybe. Providing I manage to convince him I *can* tidy them up."

She leaned toward the mirror and examined her reflection pensively. "To do that you've got to convince yourself first."

"Perhaps Manders will do it for me," he said.

But Doctor Manders had no easy solutions to offer. He listened thoughtfully while, over dinner, Laurie recounted the day's discoveries, then without expressing an opinion, he turned to Carol and asked her what she made of it.

She frowned. "I think he's gone about as far as it's possible to go without putting the whole thing on an official level. Jim won't talk unless he's made to, and the only people who could track down Nadler and his friends—supposing they're still in this country—are the police. Laurie can hardly be expected to follow up the Benoit connection by himself and what else is there left?"

"There *is* still one thing," said Laurie. "The obvious one."

"What's that?"

"Well, the M.I.S."

To his astonishment it was Manders who nodded. "You're right, of course," he said.

Laurie blenched. "You can't expect *me* to . . ."

"No, no. This one is for me."

Laurie and Carol exchanged glances. "What will you do?" asked Laurie.

Manders picked up his wineglass and revolved it by its stem. "Publish my report on Lynn's case."

"You mean they'd *let* you?"

"I'm quite certain they wouldn't. So I shall take good care not to inform them beforehand. With a modicum of good luck they'll find themselves faced with a *fait accompli.*"

"But won't they . . . won't *you* . . . ?"

"Lose my job. On the whole I doubt it. It rather depends on the sort of impact my report makes. If it's big enough, who knows, it may even gain me promotion."

Laurie eyed him quizzically. "But couldn't you have done that six weeks ago?"

"That's right," Manders agreed, and smiled faintly.

"Yet you didn't."

"I didn't know then what I know now."

"The Benoit connection, you mean?"

"That too," said Manders.

"You mean there's something else?"

Manders nodded.

"Can't you tell us?"

The Doctor looked from one to the other and then gave an infinitesimal shrug. "You understand that this will have to be *absolutely* confidential?"

They both nodded, wide-eyed.

"I underline this purely for your own safety," he

continued, "because if what I suspect proves to be true, then what I'm about to tell you may eventually put you in a position of very real danger. Is that understood?"

"Yes," they said.

"And you still want me to go on?"

Again they nodded.

Manders sighed faintly. "Before we came out this evening I told you I had two phone calls to make. One of them was to my brother Harold who is on the permanent staff of the Home Office. Without letting him know what I was after I got him to confirm that at the time the M.I.S. took us over they also took over several rather obscure sub-departments of the Ministry of Defense."

He paused and took a sip at his wine. "What had given me my lead was that ampoule you brought in yesterday. This morning I put Brenda on trying to track it down. It seemed a pretty forlorn hope, but by four o'clock this afternoon she'd succeeded in tracing it. The last two letters of its serial code were KS. It turned out to be one of a batch of ten thousand made up under Government contract by a Dutch firm called *Köbler & Stassen* for one of those very peculiar sub-departments which now form part of our organization."

"So you *have* found out what the stuff is!" exclaimed Laurie.

"Don't you believe it," said Manders. "In fact the only reason we found out as much as we did was because we're now part of the M.I.S. ourselves."

"But surely you know which department it was for?"

"One which apparently concerns itself with something called 'Psychological Strategy.' "

"And what the hell's that?"

"You tell me," said Manders. "Harold did a bit of

ferreting around but couldn't discover anything of consequence. It's apparently Top Secret. He *was* able to give me a name though." He delved into an inner pocket and produced a scrap of paper. 'The presiding genius—if that's the right term—of the Department of Psychological Strategy is a certain Colonel Magobion."

Laurie's head jerked up. *"Who?"*

"Magobion," repeated Manders. "Why? Have you heard of him?"

Laurie frowned and seemed to be groping in the shadowy recesses of his memory. "Magobion," he muttered, and again: "Magobion." Suddenly he shivered violently and felt a cold dew of sweat break out all over his body.

Carol regarded him apprehensively. "Are you feeling all right?"

He contrived a pale grin. "A bit odd," he whispered and suddenly screwed his eyes tight shut and then opened them very wide.

Manders leaned forward across the table and waved his hand, palm flat, before Laurie's ashen face. "Extraordinary," he murmured.

"What is it?" whispered Carol. "What's the matter with him?"

Manders peered into Laurie's face. The pupils of the eyes were hugely dilated as though by belladonna. As he gazed into them he saw them beginning to contract. Laurie blinked again, glanced around him and touched the wooden tabletop, at first hesitantly, then with increasing pressure. "What was it?" he demanded. "Something's happened."

"Tell us," said Manders curiously.

Laurie licked his lips. "Magobion," he muttered. "Piers Magobion."

"What about him?"

Fine droplets of sweat were pricked out across

Laurie's forehead. "I don't know," he said and shuddered violently.

Manders picked up the bottle of Beaujolais and poured more wine into Laurie's glass. "Knock that back," he ordered, "and then tell us how you come to know his name is 'Piers'."

Laurie raised the wine to his lips and drank. As he set the glass down again he said: "But I *don't* know. How could I? I'm sure I've never heard the name before in my life."

"You must have forgotten," said Manders. "It often happens, you know."

Laurie shook his head. "It wasn't like that," he insisted. "Not like that at all."

"Then tell us what it *was* like," suggested Manders mildly.

"It was as though—" Laurie began hesitantly and then stopped.

"Yes?"

Laurie's eyes were utterly bewildered. "As though it had *happened*," he muttered. "And it was happening *again*. But this time it was . . . different somehow." His gaze seemed to lurch and recover itself. He half-turned and stared incredulously at Carol. "Billie," he whispered. "You're Billie."

It was Carol's turn to gape. "Who on earth told you that?"

Manders' glance flickered from one to the other.

"What does he mean?" he demanded. "Who's 'Billie'?"

"I am," said the mystified Carol. "At least I *was*. My father used to call me 'Billie.' But it was only a pet name. No one's used it for years."

"You must have told him," said Manders.

"Don't be ridiculous!" she retorted. "I only *met* him today!"

75

The Doctor shook his head, signifying total mystification.

"But how did *he* know it?" she insisted. "What's going on?"

"Since you ask me," said Manders, regarding Laurie thoughtfully, "I'd say we'd just witnessed some sort of post-hypnotic manifestation—apparently triggered by the name 'Magobion.' Are you *quite* sure you've never heard it before?"

Laurie frowned and shook his head slowly. "Who is he?" he said.

Manders shrugged. "I know no more than you do —less, if his first name really is 'Piers'."

"How can we find out?"

"In the past it would have been simple enough," said Manders. "We'd just have looked him up in the Army List. Nowadays it's not so easy. I daresay Harold could find out somehow, but it'll take time."

"What did you say that department was called?" asked Laurie. "Psychological Warfare?"

"Strategy," said Manders. "Psychological Strategy."

"And what's that?"

"Propaganda?" suggested Carol.

"Perhaps," said Manders.

"You don't think so?"

Manders shook his head.

"Well, what then?"

"I really don't know," said the Doctor. "But I don't think the label signifies very much. Some very peculiar ships are sailing under flags of convenience these days."

"Such as what?" she asked.

" 'Hydrophonic Communications,' for one. In simple words—talking whale talk."

Carol giggled. "You suppose Lynn was having a go at that when Jim fished her out of the river?"

"Who knows?" smiled Manders.

Laurie gazed at the Doctor. "Lynn," he murmured. "Maybe *she's* the connection."

"How do you mean?"

"Well, that poltergeist stuff . . . No, it's too crazy."

"Yes, it is, isn't it?" agreed the Doctor. "But does it look quite so crazy when I tell you that, to my certain knowledge, during the past fifteen years at least four governments have been conducting research into drug-induced telepathy?"

"You mean you think *she*—"

"No, no," said Manders hastily. "Don't misunderstand me. All I'm saying is that you may not be wrong to look for some sort of connection there."

"Are you implying that whatever drug these Strategy people are working on has turned out to be addictive?" demanded Carol.

" 'Implying' " is perhaps a little too strong."

"And Benoit? How does he fit in?"

"Well, I suppose it *might* be possible to establish some sort of a link between Carouge in Geneva and *Köbler & Stassen* in Amsterdam. They're certainly both subsidiaries of *Mondiale*."

"Hey, *yes!*" she breathed. "Now we're *really* getting somewhere!"

A waiter approached their table and murmured something in the Doctor's ear. He nodded, pushed back his chair and said: "There's a phone call for me. I'll be back in a moment. Order coffee, will you? Black for me."

When Carol had placed the order she turned to Laurie. "Now tell me how you knew I was called 'Billie.' "

He shook his head. "I'm sorry, Carol. I can't. I just *knew*, that's all."

"You expect me to believe that?" she protested.

"How can I?" he said unhappily. His eyes seemed to focus on some point far beyond her. "There *was*

77

something," he murmured. "A long time ago. When I was a kid. I'd forgotten all about it . . ."

"Well, go on," she prompted. "Tell me."

"It was a sort of dream I had," he muttered uneasily.

"What about?"

"That's just it," he said, "I can't *remember*. But it was something to do with going fishing."

"Fishing!"

He groped back into his memory, fumbling among the elusive wisps of recollection, but it was as though the very act of reaching for them wafted them beyond his grasp. He shook his head, perplexed and frustrated.

"When *was* this?" she asked.

He shrugged. "Oh, years ago now. The summer of '87."

She gave him an odd look. "You're sure it was '87?"

He nodded. "July '87."

"My father died in '87. It was the last time anyone ever called me 'Billie.' "

"Billie," he whispered, so softly she barely heard him, and again his eyes darkened with his effort to remember.

"And Magobion?" she said. "Where does he come in?"

He shivered and she heard him say, quite tonelessly, *"Kill Magobion."*

Carol gulped. *"What* did you say?"

"Huh?" Laurie blinked. "I didn't say anything."

"You did! *You* said—well, I *thought* you said—'Kill Magobion.' "

" 'Kill Magobion?' "

"That's right."

"Billie, I—"

78

"Oh, for God's sake stop calling me that! You're giving me the creeps!"

Laurie buried his face in his hands. "I feel lousy," he said.

"Sick?"

He nodded. "And scared too. What did Manders mean about post-hypnotic suggestion?"

"I don't know what he meant," she said.

The waiter returned with their coffee and, while he was in the process of distributing it, Manders reappeared and took his place at the table. "Wheels within wheels within wheels," he announced enigmatically. "That was your boss."

"Major Gross?"

Manders nodded.

"But I was supposed to be contacting *him!*"

"It seems that will no longer be necessary. You've been relieved."

"Relieved! Just like that? Why?"

"The M.I.S. moves in a mysterious way it's—"

"The M.I.S.! You're not serious!"

"Well, someone has brought pressure to bear. As from now you're off this inquiry. In fact you're on leave."

"I don't believe it!"

"It's perfectly true." Manders reached out for the sugar and smiled slyly. "Ken seemed to think you were due for a fortnight's end-of-course furlough."

"Well, yes, I know I am," said Laurie.

"They tell me Geneva's very attractive at this time of the year."

"Geneva!"

"Carouge," Manders observed thoughtfully, "is almost part of Geneva."

Laurie looked across at Carol and raised his eyebrows interrogatively.

79

"A busman's holiday," pursued the Doctor glibly, "can often be extremely rewarding."

"Figuratively speaking."

"A modest honorarium would not seem out of place," murmured Manders, sipping at his coffee. "As a reward for some sterling services."

Carol said: "Would it interest anyone to know that I'm due for a week off from next Monday?"

"Excellent!" exclaimed Manders. "Then might I suggest a little continental tour?" He put down his cup and touched the tip of his left thumb with his right index finger. "You start with Paris—so delightful in the Spring—where my good friend Professor Henri Martell will, I know, be enchanted not only to offer you hospitality but also to discourse at length on the properties of certain peculiar drugs upon which he is a leading world authority. Two: Geneva and a social call upon Doctor Albert Dring, an ex-colleague of mine at present working under contract for *Mondiale*. Three: home via Amsterdam in time for the tulip festival and perhaps a brisk tour of Messrs. *Köbler & Stassen*'s very modern pharmaceutical works at Zaandam, which as we all know, is but a short trip along the canals from Haarlem."

Laurie gnawed his lip and looked at Carol.

"Does that appeal to you, Miss Kennedy?" inquired Manders.

"Does it!" she laughed. "I wonder if I could talk Chick into letting me off on Friday afternoon?"

"Is Major Gross in on this too?" asked Laurie.

"Good Lord, no!" Manders contrived to sound shocked. "Major Gross, like the trustworthy officer he is, obeys his orders to the letter." He smiled. "But none of us like beng leaned on *too* heavily."

Laurie and Carol boarded the veetol jump-jet at Battersea at 6 p.m. the following day. They touched down at the Heliport de Paris exactly one hour later, and by 8:15 were sipping aperitifs in Professor Henri Martell's apartment on the Quai D'Anjou. While they gazed down upon the barges gliding along the Seine, the white-haired Professor sat poring over the copy of Manders' report on Lynn which they had brought him. From time to time he murmured, or clicked hs tongue. Finally he removed his glasses and tapped the typescript with them. "I," he announced, "am perhaps the only man in Paris who could read what is written here without surprise. I have long suspected that it would be merely a matter of time before someone succeeded in synthesizing one of the neuronal enzymes."

"You think that's what it is?" asked Laurie.

"I think it is highly probable. But there are many of them to choose from and they are all exceedingly complex."

"But what use would it be?" inquired Carol.

"That, my dear, would presumably depend upon who was administering it—and to whom it was being administered."

"Lynn—the girl Doctor Manders calls "Catherine" —looked about sixteen years old," said Laurie.

"James appears to have arrived at a figure of seventeen and a half," said the Professor, glancing down at the report.—"He admits that to be an approximation. However, since we are considering the possibility of a synthesized enzyme, I do not think that the precise physical age is of great consequence. What would be helpful would be to know more of the subject's innate gifts—her intellectual abilities."

"How would that help?"

"It might perhaps give us an insight into the nature of this drug if we knew what those who were administering it were hoping to achieve."

Carol darted a quick look at Laurie. "Do you mean

you believe this girl was—well, a sort of scientific guinea-pig?"

"Oh yes," said Professor Martell. "Naturally, lacking evidence to the contrary, I have to assume a *willing* volunteer, but within our present terms of reference certainly a guinea-pig."

Carol flushed. "But I can't believe *that!*" she protested.

The Professor seemed surprised. "My dear young lady, I assure you that it would not be the first case by any means. Regrettable though it may be, there is today a thriving trade between the developing countries and ourselves in what is euphemistically termed "laboratory technicians." The pay is good; the conditions infinitely superior to anything they have ever known in their homelands; consequently there is no shortage of applicants."

"But this girl was English," said Laurie. "English speaking anyway."

"She spoke?"

"Before she was brought to the Center she did," he said, and sketched in briefly what he had been able to discover at Gravesend.

The Professor listened attentively, his head tilted slightly to one side. "It is, indeed, a peculiar history," he remarked. "One might almost go so far as to call it "sinister.' "

"Have you ever come across another case like it, Professor?" asked Carol.

"Never. It is unique in my experience. And it is precisely that aspect which I find so disturbing. You see, my dear, it appears to me that what we are confronted with here is not some exotic new hallucinogen but a substance which, besides being addictive, has the property of releasing what, for want of a better term, I must call the latent psychic energies of the addict. Now the only neuronal enzymes I can think of that might conceivably be capable of producing some such effect as this would be those of the cholinesterase group, whose molecular structure has hitherto proved far too complex to be synthesized on anything approaching a commercially viable scale. Yet you tell me that this ampoule you discovered was one of a batch of ten thousand! The conclusions one must draw are, to say the least, alarming."

"But why should anyone want to do it?" demanded Carol. "What *use* would it be?"

"That would presumably depend upon whether the effect—the released energies—could be contained and controlled," observed the Professor.

"Could they?" asked Laurie.

Martell gave an expressive Gallic shrug. "We know so little about them. Psychokinesis has been permitted official existence only since the results of the Bauker/Harland experiments were published in 1982. Generally speaking it still remains the dark continent. But I should hesitate to say that nobody has carried on from where Bauker and Harland left off." He tapped the paper he was still holding. "Especially now that I have read this."

"Then you don't think that poltergeist stuff was just a weird side-effect?"

"I have no way of telling. Perhaps. Perhaps not."

"But if it wasn't," said Carol, "what are they hoping to do?"

"I wonder," mused the Professor. "The military mind is in some respects quite remarkably deficient in subtlety. It is structured to think only in terms of aggression and defense—of allies and enemies. In my experience it is a mentality capable of great ingenuity but one which remains essentially simplistic. So, if what James tells me is correct—and why should I doubt it?—then I might just suppose this unfortunate child to be a part of some novel *diablerie militaire,* designed perhaps to combat or to influence sophisticated electronic structures. That is, of course, pure supposition on my part, you understand."

Both Carol and Laurie gazed at him blankly striving to come to terms with a concept so outlandish that it seemed to have strayed out of the sci-fic. T.V. serials of their childhood. Beside it even Manders' talk of drug-induced telepathy and hydrophonic communication seemed as straight-forward as bows and arrows.

Laurie was the first to recover his powers of speech. "Do you *really* think that's possible?" he asked.

"Conceivable, certainly," said Martell. "Whether it has taken that particular form I am hardly in a position to say. However, I can assure you that the latent powers of the human psyche have been a major field for weapons research for a number of years. It is a deplorable fact, but it *is* a fact nonetheless."

He rose to his feet, smiled at them, and said: "My children, there is a delightful little restaurant I have recently discovered which calls itself *"Le Couvre-Plat Flottant."* It will give me the greatest pleasure to introduce you to it. I always say there is nothing quite like good food for helping to regain one's sense of perspective. After that, if you are agreeable, I shall be delighted to show you something of my still beautiful city."

Laurie and Carol spent two days in Paris and, as Manders had hinted, they learned more about the wilder hinterlands of modern drug research than previously they had ever believed to exist. Henri Martell proved to be a virtually inexhaustible information bank who took an impish delight in "making them gasp and stretch their eyes." "Since we discovered the true function of the glia," he said, "we have uncovered 'selves' that our parents would hardly have dared to dream about. There is, for instance, one very mysterious substance which has the extraordinary property of allowing one to, as it were, swim along what old Carl Jung would have called "the Oceanic stream." By so doing one makes contact with all the separate individual evolutionary stages which have gone to make up the monster we know as *homo sapiens.*

"There are substances in an active state of preparation which will, before very long, undoubtedly enable information to be injected directly into our memory cells and provide us with instant information. Indeed, I myself, have taken a not inconsiderable part in their development.

"There is even one drug, to which Jean Roland, its creator, has given the name *"prozatamine"* and which —between ourselves—is still in a highly experimental stage. This, he claims, may one day prove to have the power of enabling one to skip backward in time and make contact with one's earlier self. However," he added with a twinkling smile, "personally I reserve my doubts as to whether anyone will ever do so. Nevertheless it may happen. And so, you see, your little Lynn is by no means the only voyager upon uncharted seas."

From Paris Laurie and Carol traveled on to Geneva by the TransEuropean Monorail Express—still, after twenty years the justifiable pride and joy of the S.N.C.F. During the journey they discussed, among other things, whether they should rent a double room or two singles when they got to Switzerland. "What it boils down to is this," said Carol. "Do you find me sexually attractive?"

Laurie scratched his chin and grinned, "Yes," he said, "as a matter of fact I do. Very."

"Well, that settles that then," she said. "I wasn't sure whether you were a homosexual. I often find I'm attracted to homosexuals."

"I see. I suppose I could take that as a compliment."

"You can if you want to. I'd certainly like to go to bed with you right now. But then trains sometimes do have that effect on me."

"Oh," said Laurie. "You mean you think you might change your mind when it stops?"

"We'll have to see, won't we?" she laughed. Personally I doubt it, but you never know."

They found themselves a modest 60 storey hotel on the northern shore of the dead lake and within minutes of being shown up to their room Carol effectively demonstrated that she had not changed her mind. "That was really great," she sighed. "It's so nice to do it with someone who isn't kinky. My last partner insisted on wearing an aqua-suit. I felt like that princess in the fairy tale who finds she's landed herself with a frog."

Laurie laughed, disentangled himself, and gave her a thoughtful, lingering kiss on the breast. "I suppose we ought to be thinking about getting in touch with Herr Doktor Dring."

Carol yawned. "There'll be plenty of time for that later. We *are* supposed to be on holiday, remember?"

"I hadn't forgotten. Hey, you're a natural blonde!"

"Don't say you've only just noticed."

"Passion must have blinded me," he chuckled. "It's very becoming."

She grinned and reached out for him. "You've been pretty becoming yourself," she murmured. "And something tells me you're going to be coming some more very shortly."

Just before six Laurie succeeded in persuading her to video-phone Doctor Dring. It had been his intention to make an appointment for the two of them to call on the Doctor the next morning but Dring insisted on their dining with him that very evening. "I will collect you myself," he said. "Let us meet in the foyer in half an hour."

The moment they emerged from the expressavator vestibule a man in a dark blue uniform hurried over to them from the reception desk. *"M'sieu Linton?* (he pronounced it 'Lan-ton'), *Mam'selle Kennedy? Suivez-moi, s'il vous plaît."* He turned on his heel and strode briskly off in the direction of the main entrance.

Laurie and Carol shrugged and followed him. As they reached the portico they saw drawn up below them a long black and silver vehicle of the type known popularly as a "land boat." The windows were of tinted glass and it was impossible to get more than the vaguest impression of anyone inside. Seeing it had the effect of making them both feel improperly dressed.

As they descended the steps the chauffeur swung open the rear door. Carol climbed in followed by Laurie. The door closed on them with a solid thud and a click. "Doctor Dring?" said Carol.

A large man with a thick mat of iron gray hair and dark glasses who was sitting in the back of the car leaned forward and pressed a button which activated a speaker. "Gex," he said.

There was hardly a sound as the car slid away toward the autoroute. The man turned to Carol. "There has been a slight change of plan," he said. "I felt it was time we had a little talk."

"You're not Doctor Dring!"

The man chuckled. "No," he admitted. "I am not Dring."

"Who are you?"

"I am Gabriel Benoit."

Laurie gulped.

"Ah, I see my name is familiar to you, Mister Linton. I am flattered. And how did you come to learn of it?"

"Where are you taking us?"

"That depends," said Benoit.

"What d'you mean?"

Benoit sighed. "I hope I shall be able to persuade you to co-operate with me. You see, Mister Linton, I too am becoming—how shall I put it?—decidedly intrigued by the activities of a certain Colonel Magobion."

"You know about *him!*"

"Not as much as I should like to, certainly. But something, yes."

The car drifted out into the express lane and Laurie heard the rising whisper of its jet. He glanced at Carol but if he had hoped to get some guidance from her he was disappointed. She gave a tiny twitch of her eyebrows as much as you say: "It's you who've got us into this." "What do you know about Magobion?" he said.

"The Colonel appears to be an ambitious man," said Benoit. "Do you find ambition an attractive quality, Mister Linton?"

"Not very," said Laurie. "It all depends."

Benoit chuckled fatly. "A very English reply. And how about Miss Kennedy?"

Carol shrugged. "What sort of ambition?" she asked.

"The usual one," said Benoit. "Power."

"What sort of power?"

"The power to control human destiny, Miss Kennedy. In my experience it is an appetite which grows as it feeds."

"You've met him, have you?" asked Laurie.

"I? No." He smiled. "Our paths have not yet crossed."

"Then why are you so interested in him?"

"That, my dear Mister Linton, is what is known as a leading question. Let us strike a bargain. I will tell you why *I* am interested in Colonel Magobion if *you* will tell me why NARCOS is interested in him."

"What makes you think we are?"

"Oh, come now, Mister Linton. I am too old for games. You surely will not expect me to believe that it is pure coincidence that takes you and Miss Kennedy from Doctor Manders, to Professor Martell, to Doctor Dring, and finally—am I not right—to *Köbler & Stassen?*"

"Well, well," said Laurie. "Someone's been busy."

Benoit shrugged. "I make it my business to know such things. Yours is a journey which can have but one ending, and we are both aware what that is."

"Since you know so much," said Laurie, "you obviously know the answer to your own question."

"But I do not, Mister Linton."

Laurie tapped his lower lip with the knuckle of his thumb. "And what would you say if I told you that NARCOS hasn't got the faintest official interest in your Colonel Magobion."

"Naturally I should not believe you."

Laurie nodded. "O.K.," he said, "that's your affair. Now—speaking entirely for myself, you understand—I *am* interested in him."

"For yourself, of course. I understand, Mister Linton."

"I wonder if you do?" murmured Laurie.

The car having edged back into the slow lane was now swooping down into an underpass prior to heading inland toward the snow-crested mountains.

"And why *are* you interested in Colonel Magobion, Mister Linton?"

They plunged into the gloomy tunnel under the autoroute. For an instant Laurie felt that he was drowning, that some malignant force was dragging him down irrestibly into a world of shadows. *Kill Magobion.* He shuddered, closed his eyes and struck upward for the surface. The sunlight drew him into its arms. "Because I believe he's dangerous," he muttered.

"Ah," murmured Benoit. "Now you are interesting me. Please explain."

"That's just what I can't do," said Laurie. "It's only a hunch."

" 'Hunch?' What is that?"

"Un preséntiment," said Carol.

Benoit nodded. "About K-12?"

Laurie felt Carol's elbow nudge into his ribs. "Could be," he said carefully.

"What else?" said Benoit. "But I am a little surprised that NARCOS should concern itself with so—" he paused as though searching for the word he wanted "—so exotic a substance as K-12."

"Even though you're concerned with it?" retorted Laurie.

"Touché!" chuckled Benoit. "But tell me, Mister Linton, what have you learned about its peculiar properties?"

"I know it's addictive."

"Indeed?"

"Well, it is, isn't it?"

"Not perhaps in quite the sense you imagine."

"What other sense is there?"

"There is a sense in which the music of Johann Sebastian Bach might be considered addictive. Once heard by certain ears no other music will satisfy that particular spiritual hunger. But one does not *have* to listen to Bach."

Laurie stared at him and slowly shook his head. "I don't believe you."

Benoit shrugged. "K-12," he said. "Do you know what the "K" represents?"

"No."

"Kállos."

"So? What does it mean?"

"It is the Aancient Greek word for 'beauty,' Mister Linton."

"Go on."

"K-12 has been called *The Gateway to Paradise*."

"Not exactly original, is it?"

"No," agreed Benoit. "But supposing it were true. . . ."

Like a faint, troublesome echo Laurie recalled Doctor Manders' voice saying: *"Something tells me that kid's found the pot of gold at the rainbow's end."* He frowned. "And Magobion?" he said.

"Ah, Mister Linton, as your Shakespeare says, there is the rub. The greedy Colonel has chosen to place *Kállos* under a strict security ban."

"Presumably he's a Bach enthusiast," Laurie suggested ironically.

"Bach? Ah ha, yes. That could be so."

"You don't sound convinced."

"Mister Linton, I feel the time has come to explain my position a little more fully. I am, as you probably know, an executive director of *Mondiale*. A vital role in the development of K-12 was undertaken by one of our scientists—a certain Doctor Karl Strübe—working with a team of British scientists. Strübe was under long-term contract to *Mondiale,* who loaned his services to Colonel Magobion for the duration of the project. The contract we signed with the British made it a condition of Strübe's employment that all discoveries made by the team should be shared mutually between us. Doctor Strübe returned to us last year. Unfortunately we discovered that he had suffered a—how shall I say it?—a 'limited lapse of memory?'—which effectively prevented him from communicating any information about his recent research. Naturally we were deeply distressed, particularly since we had excellent reason for believing that the whole K-12 project had proved quite remarkably successful. Colonel Magobion was not helpful. He insisted that Strübe was perfectly at liberty to communicate whatever he wished to *Mondiale* and therefore his own legal obligations were fulfilled."

Laurie nodded. "And presumably he was within his legal rights otherwise you'd certainly have done something about it long before this."

"The case is still under consideration by the International Court," admitted Benoit gloomily, "but in essence you are correct."

"And you think Magobion is responsible for Strübe's loss of memory?"

"Mister Linton, I am certain of it."

Carol glanced around at Benoit. "But if *Köbler & Stassen* have been making up this stuff for the M.I.S., surely the formula must be accessible to *Mondiale?*"

"Alas, no, Miss Kennedy. The contract to which you refer was placed under strict NATO security. Furthermore, *Köbler & Stassen* is the most highly automated pharmaceutical plant in Europe. This is undoubtedly why it was chosen. The K-12 formula was fed into the computers by members of Colonel Magobion's own staff and all records were erased after the batch was completed. All we were able to learn was the serial numbers on the ampoules."

"Ingenious," murmured Laurie. "And so what's your next step?"

Benoit's gold-banded fingers tapped out a rapid little tattoo on the upholstered arm-rest. "It occurred to me, Mister Linton, that once the true nature of the situation had been explained to you, you might be prepared to assist us."

"*Me!*"

"NARCOS has means of access which are denied to lesser mortals."

"*Civil* access, maybe. Not military."

"*Mondiale* can be a very generous employer, Mister Linton."

Laurie turned his head and gazed out of the sepia-tinted window. They were climbing up through the pine forest, flicking in and out of the sun-bright clearings and tunnels of somber shadow. He wondered what Benoit's real interest was in K-12. Perhaps he too was just another Bach enthusiast. It seemed somewhat unlikely. "How generous?" he asked curiously.

"For each ampoule of K-12, we are prepared to pay you twenty thousand Swiss francs. For a copy of the formula itself two hundred thousand."

It sounded a lot of money. "And I'm supposed to wander up to Colonel Magobion and ask him to hand it over?"

Benoit smiled. "I do not think that even someone as beautiful as Miss Kennedy could persuade him to do that."

"Then how?"

"Mister Linton, I believe you to be a young man of considerable determination and resource. I know also that the Department of Psychological Strategy has its research establishment at a place called Gowers Marsh on the Thames estuary. Would it not be possible for you to effect an entry to this place on the pretext that you are following up a line of investigation for NARCOS?"

Laurie's heart tripped. "Whereabouts on the Thames estuary?"

"Gowers Marsh. It is near Southend, I believe."

"Opposite Gravesend?"

Behind the dark lenses of his glasses Benoit's eyes seemed to flicker. My knowledge of your local geography is not very extensive, Mister Linton."

"Liar," thought Laurie. "I'll bet you've had the place under twenty-four hour watch ever since Jim tried to drum up that stuff for Lynn." Aloud he said: "I'd have to check on your story first. You realize that?"

"Of course, Mister Linton. You would decline

sharply in my estimation if you failed to do so. But I assure you I am telling the truth."

"What's the truth about an iceberg?" retorted Laurie. "What shows above the surface or what's hidden beneath it?"

Benoit chuckled, then leaned forward, pressed the speaker button and murmured some instruction to his chauffeur. Outside the window a signboard bearing the single word *'GEX'* flicked past. "It has been a pleasure making your acquaintance, Mister Linton. I shall arrange for us to keep in touch."

Laurie glanced sideways. "What happens now?"

Benoit spread his hands. "Now? Why you enjoy the hospitality of Doctor Dring and his good lady."

"Dring?"

"But of course. Did you not know? He lives here in Gex. I arranged with him that I should pick you up and bring you to him. What else could you have supposed?"

Carol broke into a wild giggle which had still not completely subsided when the huge car drew up outside a wrought-iron gate on the outskirts of the village. The chauffeur climbed out, trotted around and unfastened the rear door. Benoit held out his hand. "Forgive me if I do not accompany you to the door," he said, "but I have another appointment in Geneva. *Au revoir,* Miss Kennedy. *Au revoir,* Mister Linton."

It was after midnight when Laurie and Carol were returned to their hotel by the amiable Doctor Dring. Insofar as he had been able to he had confirmed Benoit's story about Karl Strübe. "You must, however, realize that Gabriel does not confide in me a great deal," he had told them. "All that I am telling you is common knowledge in *Mondiale.* I know nothing of the precise nature of Strübe's research."

94

"Frankly I'd trust Benoit about half as far as I can spit," observed Laurie when he and Carol reached the sanctuary of their room on the forty-seventh floor.

"You can say that again for me," she agreed. "What do you bet we've been bugged? I'll swear someone's been through here while we were out."

They spent the next five minutes inspecting the room and to Carol's triumphant disgust discovered a microtransmitter taped to the underside of one of the twin beds. "If that had been there when we first arrived they might have heard something worth hearing," she growled, opening the window and shying the offensive eavesdropper out into the night.

"At least you have to grant Gabriel a certain style," laughed Laurie. "I didn't even recognize him."

"Nor me," she admitted. "The wig made him look about twenty years younger. I'll have to revise our records when we get back."

"I wish I'd thought to ask him what he'd managed to get out of Jim," said Laurie. "Do you suppose he'd have told me?"

"Probably. If he'd thought it would help."

"Gowers Marsh," he murmured. "It's a pity I haven't got a map."

"We can look for one in the morning. Come and unzip me."

Laurie drew the plastic tab downward from nape to tail. Carol squirmed out of her dress like a slender, pink and gold larva and fumbled for the fastenings of her bra.

"I wonder how Lynn *did* get into the water," he mused.

"She fell off a boat," said Carol, dropping the scrap of lace on to the bed and slipping her hands into the waistband of her briefs. "The man said so. It happens every day."

95

"You don't believe that, do you?"

"That she dropped off a boat? How should I know?" She padded over to the dressing table, opened her toilet case and took out a curved tortoiseshell comb. Then she ducked her head, gathered up the tassels of her barley-yellow hair and pinned them deftly on the top of her head. "I'm going to have a shower," she announced. "Care to join me?"

Laurie's preoccupied frown relaxed into a slow grin. "Has anyone ever told you you're not unattractive?"

"I was beginning to wonder how long it would be before it registered," she chuckled. "Come on. I just *love* being soaped."

But in spite of the ozonic shower and the affectionate wrestling match which followed it, it was a long time before Laurie slept. He lay open-eyed in the darkness, listening enviously to Carol's calm breathing, while his own restless thoughts zig-zagged back and forth over the events of the past few days like a frustrated fox-hound questing for a lost trail. And ever and again he found himself running head foremost into a blank wall on which was scrawled in letters ten feet high the single word *Magobion*. He knew that the name was associated in some inexplicable way with that mysterious incident in his childhood which had long since been buried and forgotten, and he realized too that there must be some part of him that did not *want* to remember. It was as though he were swimming against some dark, invisible tide which was determined to prevent him ever coming safe to shore. And yet the tide was *within himself*. Beside him in the shadows Carol shifted restlessly and muttered something inaudible. "Billie," he whispered in the darkness. "Billie?"

He heard the rhythm of her breathing change abruptly into a rapid and shallow panting. "Billie?" he repeated softly. "What is it?"

96

Suddenly Carol twisted violently beneath the covers, flung out an arm and cried out: "NO! NO!" A second later she jerked upright and screamed aloud.

He snatched at the switch of the bedside light.

Her eyes were staring wide with shock, her mouth hanging loosely open. A thin, silvery snail-track of saliva was dribbling down her chin. As if from a long and fearful journey her horror-struck gaze seemed to come slowly back to him. "O God," she whispered, "O God, it was a dream. Just a dream."

He crouched beside her and held her to him, feeling her shudder as the shock waves ebbed through her and away. "What was it?" he whispered. "What happened?"

"Laurie?"

He stroked her warm, bare shoulder with his lips. "It's all right," he murmured. "It's all right now. You had a dream, that's all."

She drew in a huge gulping breath and let it out in a long, tremulous sigh. "I thought that was all over and done with," she groaned. "I'm sorry. Did I wake you up?"

"I wasn't asleep," he said. "Can't you tell me what it was?"

She loosened herself from his arms, lay back and covered her eyes with her hand. "It was the dying dream," she said in a weary, exhausted voice.

" 'Dying dream'?"

The tip of her tongue emerged and edged its way along her lower lip. "I used to have it a lot," she said. "Always the same one. Then after Daddy died I didn't have it any more."

"Can't you tell me about it?"

"Must I?"

Laurie leaned over her and saw the reason she had covered her eyes. Two large tears had gathered, brimmed over, and were tickling slowly down toward

97

her ears. He extended his fingers and brushed them lightly away. "I think it'll help," he said.

She seemed to consider this for a while. "It's always the same," she sighed. "I'm in this sort of truck driving down a long, long road. There's a lake too, with sailing boats on it. And there's something else, but I can never remember it properly when I wake up. Then we come to another road—a motorway, I think—and we drive along this. We're going faster and faster until we're in a sort of cutting with high rock walls. There's a big lorry ahead. Two of them. We pass the first. And . . . and. . . ."

Laurie touched her wrist and felt it trembling. "What happens then? he murmured.

"Then?" she echoed dully. "The second lorry swerves out and Steve brakes and then we're flying off the road toward the rocks and the world's all upside down. That's when I wake up." She drew back her hand and brushed it across her wet face. "I wake up because I'm dead," she said.

Laurie stared at her. "Where is this place? Do you know?"

She shook her head dumbly.

"And Steve? Who's Steve?"

"He's driving the truck."

"But who is he?"

"Steve Rowlands, I think."

"The chap at the office?"

She nodded.

"In that dream," he said, "you're always 'Billie,' aren't you?"

"How did you know that?"

"Because I think there's someone else in that truck. Someone besides Steve."

Carol's tear-bright eyes were fixed on him in a kind of desperate entreaty. "No," she whispered. "Oh no, there's not."

"I think there *is*," he insisted. "Someone who *knows* you're Billie."

She shook her head wildly. "No!" she cried. "No! There's no one else!"

"I'm there."

"*You?*" she whispered. "Oh no, not you."

"Who then?"

"I—I don't know who. Someone. He's behind us."

"His name's Laurie, isn't it? Isn't it Billie? *Isn't it?*"

"No," she sobbed. "No it's not! It's not."

He felt sick to the very roots of his soul, hating himself for hurting her so, and afraid too of some hitherto unsuspected element within himself which had driven him to do it. "I'm sorry," he said. "I don't know what's the matter with me." He lowered his head until it was resting on her breast and he could hear her heart thudding like an engine. "I think maybe I'm going crazy," he muttered.

She lay there passively enduring his weight. "No, you're quite right," she said flatly. "It *is* you. It always has been you. I just didn't want to have to say it."

"And Steve?"

"I don't know," she sighed. "He seems to fit. Maybe it isn't him."

"Maybe it isn't any of us," he said.

"What do you mean?"

"Perhaps it's just something that *could* happen. Perhaps it *has*."

"You are crazy," she said. "How could it have happened?"

Just for a second he seemed to be standing on the threshold of the penetralium, and then the moment was gone. "I don't know," he said dully. "All I know is that something extraordinary happened to me way back there in the summer of '87 and somehow it's all coming around again. I think your dream's a part of it. And so's Magobion."

"Magobion!"

"I *had* heard his name before," he said. "At some time, some place where you were still Billie. But *why? How?*"

"Don't you ever give up?" she groaned.

"I can't, Carol. That's just it. I've *got* to go on."

"You haven't *got* to do anything."

"Yes I have," he insisted. "I've got to find Magobion."

"Oh yes?" she retorted, with a flash of her old spirit. "Who says so? Benoit?"

"It's not Benoit or anyone. It's *me.*" He suddenly heaved himself up and looked down at her. "Come with me, Carol."

"Are you out of your *mind?*" she wailed. "We've only just *arrived* for Christ's sake!"

"Then you won't?"

"Have a heart, Laurie! It's your obsession not mine. Besides I'm too tired to think straight any more."

"You're right," he said. "I've gone and got myself hooked on Magobion." He lowered his face and kissed her salty mouth. "Forget I ever said it," he murmured.

Next morning Carol almost succeeded in persuading herself that the events of the night had not really happened. Laurie made no reference to them and when, over a late breakfast, she suggested they might hire a *Waterfly* and explore the lake he agreed enthusiastically. "There's just one thing I want to do first," he said. "It shouldn't take long."

"What's that?"

"Get hold of a map."

"Can't it wait till this afternoon?"

"Probably it could," he agreed. "But *I* can't."

"Oh, damn you, Laurie Linton," she said. "Damn you, damn you, *damn* you!"

"Every addict needs his fix," he grinned. "Come and help me look for mine."

The map, when they eventually tracked one down, showed Gowers Marsh to lie on the north shore of the Thames estuary some ten miles downstream of Gravesend. The scale was too small to mark the location of any buildings, but the letters "N.R." informed them that the area had been designated a nature reserve. "Does that satisfy you?" asked Carol.

Laurie shrugged. "For the time being. It's further from Gravesend than I'd expected, but then we don't know exactly where Jim found her, do we?"

"And what does the great detective intend to do now?"

He laughed. "Wasn't there some talk of hiring a *Waterfly?*"

An hour later they clambered aboard a frail, twin-hulled ephemera and shook out the sail of pink, translucent gossamer. As the breeze nuzzled into it they ghosted out from the shelter of the marina on to the blue waters beyond. Within seconds they were skittering across the twinkling surface, the twin ribbons of their wake creaming out behind them, one among thousands of similar craft all glittering and darting hither and thither in the warm spring sunshine. Beneath them the exhausted lake lay dead and sterile to its uttermost depths, but its surface still sustained the exotic and alien life of the creatures whose selfishness had contrived to poison it.

Carol piloted them up as far as Yvoire where they disembarked and had lunch. While they were eating she chose to tell Laurie something of her life's history. "My father always wanted me to be a doctor," she said, "and I thought I wanted to be one too, but after he was killed I realized the idea had died with him. There just didn't seem to be any real point. Yet I still

101

feel guilty from time to time—as though his shade is shaking its head over me."

Laurie nodded. "Dad had plans for me too. He's an engineer. But it's not for me. What made you choose NARCOS?"

"I'm not really sure. I suppose, in a way, I saw it as a sort of compromise—a superstitious genuflection toward Daddy's spirit. He was a great believer in service to humanity."

"He was a doctor himself, was he?"

"Oh no, he was a parson. He was a lot of other things too, but professionally speaking he was a pastor of human souls."

"Are you his only child?"

"I am now," she said. "My brother was killed in the same plane crash as Daddy."

"Good God! That must have been terrible!"

"It was," she said simply. "When it happened I thought it was the end of the world. But life goes on, you know. And then, one day, you discover you've somehow managed to pick up the pieces and stick them together again. You don't quite know how it's happened, but you know it has."

"And that's what you did?"

"That's what I did."

"Did it take long?"

"About two years, I think. I ran pretty wild. I just couldn't come to terms with life at all. I mean he'd been such a *good* person in the old-fashioned sense of the word, and there he was, dead. The whole thing seemed so utterly *pointless*. And then one day I was lying out on the cliffs with a boy I knew and he said to me, "When are you going to bury him, Caro?" That's when I realized that it was no use going on fighting a battle that was over before it was ever begun. Mind you, I seem to recall I tore him to pieces at the time."

"I can believe that," said Laurie.

"Do you know," she said, "you're the first person I've ever spoken to about that part of my life."

"Really?"

She nodded. "There's definitely something about you, Laurie. Something odd. But I can't make out what it is. Do you have the same effect on other girls?"

"I've never thought about it," he confessed. "But then I've never met anyone with the same sort of hole in their past that you've got in yours."

"If it comes to that," she retorted, "there seems to be a pretty odd hole in yours too."

"That's rather different."

"Is it?" she said. "I wonder."

Laurie turned his head and looked down the lake toward Lausanne. He had a curious sensation of unease and foreboding that was wholly out of keeping with the sparkling scene around him. Having purposely avoided discussing what had happened last night out of regard for Carol, he was determined not to be the first to raise it now. But he knew that he was only delaying the inevitable, and when she said: "Tell me what *did* happen in the summer of '87," he heard her almost with a sense of relief.

He turned back, looked at her, and then lifted his shoulders in the slightest possible shrug. "I saw a ghost," he said. "At least I *think* I did."

"A *ghost?*"

He nodded.

"What sort of a ghost?"

"What sorts are there?" he smiled. "It was a man. He was wearing a kind of dark blue uniform—a bit like our 'taskers,' in fact. He had some sort of metal band across here"—he touched his forehead—"gold, I think. And a sort of gold bracelet thing around each wrist."

"Did he say anything?"

He frowned. "I'm not sure. It spoke—well, its lips

103

moved. But I didn't hear anything. I know it *wanted* to talk to me . . ."

"How do you know?"

"I just do. There was something almost desperate—pleading really. I can't explain."

Carol looked at him as though she'd never really seen him before. "You really *believe* in ghosts?"

"No," he said. "That's just it. I *don't*. Yet I believe in that one. I *know* I didn't imagine it. It really *was* there."

"Where was it?"

"Beside the river. In a sort of gulley place. I was fishing."

"Is that what you were talking about the other night? When we had supper with Manders?"

Laurie gnawed his lower lip. "Not altogether," he said. "It was part of it. You see there was something else too. Later. . . ."

"You saw it again?"

"No," he said slowly. "I didn't *see* it. *I was it.*"

"You *what?*"

"I know," he said ruefully. "Mad as a hatter. But I can't explain it any other way."

"But what *happened,* Laurie?"

"Well," he said, "that same night, when I was lying in bed going back over what had happened, I suddenly sort of *saw myself* as I would have been *from his point of view.*"

"His?"

"The ghost's—the man's—call it what you like. No, wait. Let me finish. I tell you I was *there,* Carol. I was *him,* looking at *me* down this gulley. And there was something else too—something I know I've got to remember. But I can't. Not yet. And it's *that* part that you're mixed up in somehow. Well, not *you*—Billie."

"And Magobion? What about him?" she asked curiously.

104

Laurie shook his head. "Somebody said the name to me then. Or I heard it somehow."

"That's all they said? Just 'Magobion'?"

Laurie closed his eyes and drew in a deep breath. *"Kill Magobion,"* he whispered.

"They said that?"

He shook his head.

"Well, who said it?"

He opened his eyes as slowly as though each lid had its own lead weight. "I did," he said. "I said it."

"I don't know what you mean."

"But I was *him,*" he insisted. "Then, when I heard it, *I* was saying it. *I was him!* Don't you see, Carol, we'd swopped over somehow. *I'd become him!*"

"Oh Christ," she said. "Have a heart!"

"I know," he agreed. "Why do you think I've buried it for nine years? It's not exactly something you can learn to live with, is it?"

"Who else have you told?"

"No one. Well, Manders, I suppose. You were there."

"That was the first time?"

"Yes. I really didn't know how I knew the name 'Magobion'. As far as I knew I'd never heard it before in my life."

"And 'Billie'?"

"If you could tell me," he said wearily, "I'd be more than grateful."

"But what makes you so sure you didn't just imagine it all? Kids do have incredibly vivid imaginations. I know I did."

"Because if I had there'd have been other occasions, wouldn't there? Other ghosts. That was the only time ever."

"Did you ever go back there again? To where it happened?"

"Almost whenever I went fishing. Dozens of times.

105

The place is all being altered now though. They've started building a high dam across the valley. Dad's working on it. It won't be finished till 2005."

Carol shook her head. "It's one of the weirdest stories I've ever heard," she said.

"Oh, I don't know," said Laurie. "What about your dream?"

She shook her head. "Don't let's talk about that."

"Why not? Are you afraid we might find a link somewhere?"

"A link?" she echoed doubtfully. "What do you mean?"

"I'm not really sure myself," he admitted, "but I meant what I said last night. I'm convinced there's somewhere where you're Billie and I *know* you as Billie."

"That's impossible! How could there be anywhere?"

"Well, some *when,* maybe."

Carol would not have it. Perhaps the tissue covering the old wound was still too tender to withstand his probing. "I stopped being Billie nine years ago," she said, "and I'll *never* be it again! Not for you. Not for anyone. Billie's *dead,* understand? Stone *dead!*"

"She wasn't dead last night."

"You bastard!" she whispered. "Drop it, will you?"

Laurie regarded her levelly. "All right," he said. "But on one condition."

Carol said nothing.

"You help me to find Magobion."

For a moment he was sure she was going to refuse and then, very slowly and deliberately, she shook her head. "You just never, *never* give up, do you?"

"Not on this one. I can't, Carol."

"And if I tell you to go and get lost?"

He shrugged. "I *am* lost. Utterly and absolutely."

She took a single, thick strand of her long golden

hair and wound it slowly around her finger. "Did you think I'd say no?"

"I honestly didn't know what you'd do."

She gave a rueful, lopsided grin. "So much for the Haarlem Festival," she said. "Oh, what the hell. I never did care much for tulips anyway."

They caught the midnight veetol out of Geneva. It deposited them in Battersea at fifteen minutes past two. At three o'clock, creased and gummy-eyed, they tottered out of the lift on the twenty-second floor, a third of the way up the tower block in Earls' Court where Carol rented a minute apartment. "It's a real grot," she apologized, stabbing the key into the lock and twisting it. "I've never been much of a one for—*Oh my God!* . . ."

Peering over her shoulder Laurie saw what had evoked her exclamation. The room looked as though a cyclone had whirled through it. Carol gazed around, momentarily speechless, and then burst into tears. "Jesus!" she sobbed, "Oh *Jesus,* that's *all* I'm short of!"

Laurie put his arm around her and surveyed the havoc. "Come on," he said grimly, "it probably looks worse than it is." He heeled the door to behind them and, hearing the lock click, turned and glanced at it. There was no visible trace of forced entry. "Has anyone else got a key?" he asked.

Carol shook her head. "The janitor," she gulped. "I never see him."

He picked his way over to the window but it was still securely fastened from the inside, the burglar-proof screws wound right down. Nor could he see any sign of forced entry in the kitchenette. Whoever was responsible *must* have let themselves in with a key.

He went back into the main room, heaved the divan

107

back on to its feet and then picked up the easy chair. "Can you see what's missing?"

Carol wiped her eyes, retrieved a cushion shaped like an owl from beneath an upside-down occasional table, and clutching it forlornly to her breast subsided on to the divan. "I feel as if I've been raped," she mourned.

Laurie busied himself as best he could restoring some sort of order to the chaos. He unearthed a little Victorian carriage clock from a jumble of books in a corner and pressed the repeater button. The pure little chimes rang out sweetly. "No ordinary cat would have left something like that," he said. "Has anyone got it in for you?"

Carol shook her head miserably. "They must have, mustn't they?"

"But you can't think of anyone off-hand?"

"No," she said.

"Then what's missing?"

She gazed around and her look of despair slowly changed to a puzzled frown. She put down the cushion she was nursing, climbed to her feet and walked across the room where she stooped and gathered up a drawer from the wall unit. "Look!" she cried, and held up four £20 notes.

"Well, that settles that," said Laurie. "You haven't been burgled. Come on, let's put it all straight."

In less than half an hour everything was back in its place; the only casualty a single shattered wine glass which Laurie had trodden on inadvertently. Carol brought in two mugs of coffee and handed him one. "It just doesn't make sense," she said. "What could they have been after?"

"You, maybe."

"Is that meant to be funny?"

"Well, we know it wasn't your money, and what else is there?"

"But I'm *no one,* Laurie. You know that."

"I know nothing of the sort," he retorted. "In fact I'm beginning to wonder if you and I aren't two of the hottest pieces of property in the whole world."

"You're out of your mind."

"Am I? You know, Carol, I've been thinking a hell of a lot of unthinkable thoughts in the last day or two."

"And that's one of them?"

He nodded. "Do you remember what old Martell said—about some weird drug they've been experimenting with?"

"Which one?"

"I've forgotten what he called it but he said it might have the power of enabling someone to skip around in time."

"In that case 'might' is right," she chuckled.

"No, but wait! Say someone *had* discovered it? Just suppose."

"But it's im*poss*ible, Laurie. You know that."

"Martell didn't seem to think so."

"Martell!"

"All right, so it is impossible—*now.* But what about in the future?"

"One day, maybe," she conceded to humor him.

"O.K., let's make it in ten years' time then. Twenty if you like."

"What are you trying to say?"

"I'm saying that just suppose someone *did* discover such a drug. Martell didn't suggest it could make anyone travel *forward* in time, only backward. And only in a very limited and peculiar way. He said it might let someone *make contact with this earlier self! Now* do you see what I'm getting at?"

Carol breathed on to her coffee and regarded him quizzically through the feathering steam. "Go on," she said in a neutral tone. "I'm still listening."

"All right," he said. *"Now* what happens? Someone

takes this drug, goes backward in time, and meets himself years earlier. *Yet that very meeting could change the whole future!* It could even change *him!* Make him into a different person, maybe! Or take another example. Say he—the one who takes this drug—knows that a certain obscure company is going to become fantastically successful. So he tells his earlier self to buy a packet of shares in it. The moment he does it, *presto!* —his adult self's worth a fortune."

"That's ridiculous!" Carol protested. "Why, if it worked—the drug, I mean—then everybody would be on it! They'd be zooming in out of the future passing on the latest stockmarket tips to themselves. Why hasn't it happened?"

"I don't know," he said. "Maybe for the same reason that I couldn't face up to what happened in July '87. Perhaps you can't *make* contact. Or maybe there are an infinite number of possible futures and each one's different. Maybe. . . ."

"What is it?" she asked curiously. "What were you going to say?"

"Billie," he murmured. "You were Billie."

"What?"

"Yes, of *course!* That's *it!* I'm blind! *Blind!*" In his excitement he jumped up from his chair and began striding up and down the room. " '87!" he cried exultantly. "July '87! Don't you see?"

"I see you're spilling your coffee on my carpet," she observed crushingly.

He raised the mug to his lips and gulped. Then he came and squatted down beside her. "It's all beginning to make sense, Carol. *Fantastic* sense, maybe, but if you can accept the *idea,* the rest follows."

"That's nice," she said. "Well, go ahead and explain what happened to my room."

"I can't yet. But I *will.* I'm sure of it. Listen. In '87 you were going to be a doctor, weren't you? If you *had*

110

been—if your father hadn't been killed—you'd have *been* a doctor by now, and you'd still have called yourself Billie. But in '87 everything was knocked sideways. Your father was killed and you reverted to being Carol. f I'm on the right track, then I suspect all this must have happened more or less at the same moment. Some time early one morning in July. Or maybe that same evening. No, just a minute! Let me finish! Now I guess—I don't know—how could I?—that that dream of yours was something to do with *how* it happened—that *we*—you and I and this Steve character had somehow decided we'd got to make contact with me—*me as I was then*. Me as a *kid,* I mean. Yes, maybe *making* that contact was what knocked it all off sideways! Once *I'd* got the message they were done for—or their *future* was done for! . . . No, I can't follow that one through. . . . But don't you see, Carol, it *could* be the link I was talking about?"

"You're really high, aren't you?" she observed. "I wonder what you'll say when I tell you that Daddy's plane crashed at ten o'clock in the evening on July 17th?"

"I can't remember the exact day I saw my ghost," he said. "It must have been *about* then though. I wonder . . ."

"What is it?"

He shook his head. "Why *was* it so important to them? Surely they must have *known* the risk they were taking?"

"Assuming they ever did," she said.

"Oh they did," he said with complete conviction. "I'm sure of it."

"You, Mr. Linton, are what is commonly called a nut case."

"I wonder what that makes Magobion?" he mused. "Why did they have to tell *me* about *him?*"

"Oh Laurie," she sighed, "It's just an *idea.*" The

111

way she said it made it sound as though she were telling him regretfully that Santa Claus didn't really exist. "And as ideas go it's gone just about as far around the bend as anyone can push it. These things don't *happen* in real life."

"No? Well, I don't agree. I think it *did* happen. But *why*, Carol? *Why?*"

She rested her forehead wearily against his. "Please," she begged. *"Please*, Laurie, leave it alone now, or I swear to God I'll fall down on all fours and start barking."

"You're right," he grinned. "And if you've got any strength left, you can pick me up in your little pointy teeth and carry me off to bed with you."

The capsule of *Sieston* Carol had taken kept her asleep till two o'clock the following afternoon. By then the sun was slanting into the room and a *kamikaze* bluebottle was zooming back and forth, thudding up against the windowpane as though it had strict orders to die a hero's death. She opened her eyes and closed them again. "Laurie?" she murmured drowsily.

From its niche in the unit the little carriage clock pinged twice.

Carol heaved herself up on to her elbows, shook her head and blinked around. A folded sheet of notepaper was tucked inside the frame of the Derain reproduction above the electric wall fire. She kneed back the covers, padded across the room, retrieved the note and returned to the bed.

"Caro," she read, *"—do you know what that means in Italian? You're out like a light. I'm off to reconnoiter Gowers Marsh—by way of Steve Rowlands. I'm borrowing your camera for crafty disguise. Take good care of yourself. I mean that! Laurie."*

She read it through twice and each time she reached

the words "Steve Rowlands" she frowned. Then she dropped the note on to the bed, thrust her fingers deep in among the roots of her hair and scratched her scalp vigorously.

"Oh, what the hell have you got yourself mixed up in, Carol?" she muttered, and at that moment the videophone chirruped.

She wandered over to the unit, realized she was still naked, and pushed the blank-out button before lifting the receiver. "Yes?" she said. "Carol Kennedy here."

"Hi, babe!"

"Oh, hello, Steve."

"Thought I'd give you a buzz. How was the land of cows and cuckoo clocks?"

"We didn't see much of it."

"So I gather."

"You've seen Laurie, have you?"

"Linton? Sure. He beetled in at opening time. Hey, why the coy blackout your end?"

"Modesty. What did he want?"

"To borrow a pair of binoculars."

"Oh," she said, "is that all?"

"Well, no, it isn't, actually. Think of a number, Caro."

"A *number?* What is this?"

"Correction. Think of a *date*. Any date."

"Ah, I think I'm with you. How about 1987?"

"Marvelous! You and I should be on the stage."

"Stop kidding around, Steve."

"Did you tell Linton about Bimbo?"

"Bimbo? No, never. Why should I?"

"I just wondered."

"What *is* this, Steve?"

"I don't know myself. I thought *you* might."

"Well, if you'd just—"

"Linton wanted to know if anything odd had happened to me in 1987—July 1987 to be precise. Well, that was when Bimbo got smashed up."

"I didn't know."

"No? Well, it was. After all, I should know. July 17th 1987. Odd that Linton should have picked on that particular day."

"Did he say *why* he was asking?"

"No, he didn't. I thought you might know."

Carol hesitated. "It's just a line he's working on, Steve. You'll have to ask him."

"I must remember to do that some time. *Cave!* Here comes the big bad wolf. *Ciao,* beautiful."

The screen faded and died. Carol replaced the receiver, stared blankly for a moment at the window and then, shaking her head, walked through to the bathroom.

Laurie reappeared at seven o'clock. There was a ring at the bell and Carol opened the door to find herself confronting an apparition that might have stepped out of a film on jungle warfare, vintage circa. 1943. He was wearing a set of mud-plastered camouflaged denims, a bush hat, and plastic boots. Around his neck were slung an outsize pair of binoculars and her own camera.

"Christ!" she said reverently, "I simply refuse to believe it!"

Laurie grinned. "Thirty-five quid the lot. Guaranteed bird-proof at fifteen paces. Ask any ornithologist."

"And how you *stink!*"

"Not I but the mud. It's an acquired taste. You find you grow quite fond of it after a bit." He unlooped his accessories, hung them on a hook behind the door and then shucked off his boots. "I'll shove all this lot out on the balcony and have a shower."

"Was it worth the trouble?"

"Yes, I think so. I'll tell you all about it as soon as

I'm human again. Is there anything to eat? All I've had all day is a solitary bloody wimpey."

"Is the intrepid little NARCOS agent starving then?" she clucked ironically. "Oh, dear, we'll have to do something about that, won't we?"

"Aw shit," he protested. "Have a heart, Caro! I swear to God I'm just about knackered."

"All right," she relented. "It'll be ready when you are."

He kissed her briefly, divested himself of the rest of his gear and pushed it out on to the miniscule balcony with the comment: "We'll just have to keep the window shut and pray that it rains in the night."

While he was toweling himself after his shower she brought him a tumbler of whiskey and a soda siphon. She handed the glass over and fizzed soda into it. "Steve Rowlands phoned this afternoon."

"Oh yes? He told you I'd looked in, did he?"

She nodded. "What did *you* tell *him?*"

"I didn't *tell* him anything. I asked him."

"About his brother?"

"How could I? I didn't even know he *had* a brother till he told me. You knew, did you?"

"I knew he had a twin who'd been vegetabled for life in a road accident. I didn't know *when.*"

"Did you know the twin was called Stephen?"

"Stephen? You've got it back to front. His name's Bimbo."

Laurie shook his head. "Bimbo's just a nickname. Both the brothers were given the name 'Stephen'—it's a family tradition for the sons apparently. Only one of them's *called* Steve though. What do you make of that?"

"I don't know. What should I make of it?"

Laurie handed back the glass and resumed his towelling. "The Steve in your dream," he said. "When I asked you about him the other night you said he was Steve Rowlands. But if you hadn't *had* that dream for nine years, how on earth could you recognize him? I mean you hadn't even *met* Steve Rowlands when you began dreaming it, had you? How do you know it was him?"

"I don't."

"But you said you did!"

Carol shrugged. "You know how it is in dreams. You fit all sorts of odd people into them. I suppose I just happened to fit Steve into mine."

"You're *sure* that's what happened?"

Carol frowned. "Now that you mention it—no," she said. "In fact, I'm certain I'd never associated the Steve I know now with the Steve in the dream till the other night. Even when I met the real Steve for the first time I didn't *recognize* him. I suppose I just knew it *wasn't* him."

Laurie shrugged his way into his shirt. "And you can't remember anything special about the other Steve —the one in the dream? Something that would help us to identify him?"

"*Identify* him? Who with?"

"Why, with Rowland's brother, of course."

"But Bimbo's a mor—" The rest of the word never materialized.

"The penny's dropped, has it?"

Carol searched his face with her eyes, and then shivered violently. "Here, let me out," she muttered. "I want to get off."

"If I'm right," he said, "you *can't* get off. And neither can I."

"Honest to God, Laurie, I wish I'd never met you!"

"Look at me again and say that."

She raised her head, gave him an abstracted smile, then turned away and went back into the kitchenette leaving him to wrestle his way into his trousers.

Over a meal of grilled fillet-steak substitute, french fried and green salad, he told her of his day. "I bought

116

my kit at Ponders in the Strand," he said. "You've no idea the amount of gear the serious bird-watcher needs these days. A hundred quid is simply for starters. I damn nearly landed myself with a collapsible hide and a micro-decibel sound telescope and built-in recorder. As the bloke said—"Recreation is a very serious matter." When I told him I was just a beginner he got quite helpful—I suppose he thought I'd come rushing back to buy the rest of the outfit. He said I'd have to register myself as an Associate Member of the Royal Ornithological Society before I'd be allowed into a Nature Reserve. That cost me another ten quid. He sold me a map too, with all the breeding areas colored in and labeled. I bet you didn't know that Gowers Marsh is one of the only two places in the U.K. where Lindesay's avocet still breeds."

"No," admitted Carol. "You're quite right. I didn't."

"Well, it is, according to my information."

"And how about the lesser Mogobion?"

"Ah," said Laurie, "I'm coming to that sinister fowl. Don't rush me. Well, having got all my kit and credentials I tooled off to Tilbury and hired a Skeeto for the day. They charged me over the odds for that too, because they swore it had to have a special silencer in case I woke up all those broody avocets. Anyway, by half past eleven there I was, invisible from fifteen paces, chugging my way up a glorified open sewer called 'Carling's Creek.' The tide was out and there were huge evil slabs of quivery mud all over the place. I was pretty low down so I couldn't see much except reeds and about a billion common or garden seagulls. Still, I pressed on in the best gung-ho tradition, stopping every now and again to play with my camera and—"

"*My* camera!"

"I beg your pardon, *your* camera, and the binoculars

117

—just in case someone was taking a suspicious peek at me. And it's just as well I did, because after I'd gone about a mile and a half without setting eyes on a solitary living soul, a mud-covered hovercar shot out of the reeds and a couple of guards with faces like lumps of concrete wanted to know what the hell I thought I was doing.

"I decided the thing to do was to play it in character. I acted extremely haughty and blah-blahed about the Royal Orni. Soc. and Lindesay's avocet and so on and showed them my pass. 'I'm delighted to find you gentlemen are so alert,' I told them. 'Our bird sanctuaries are so few and so precious. I shall make a point of personally commending your vigilance to the Society.' 'We're nothing to do with that lot,' said one of them. 'This here's Government Property. M.I.S.' 'Goodness me!' I said. 'You don't mean to tell me that the Ministry of Internal Security has undertaken the welfare of our avocets? But this is splendid news! Surely King Charles must be behind it? His father was our patron, you know.'

"I think I almost overdid it then, but I daresay they've met some pretty way-out avocet fanciers in their time. One of them gave me back my pass and asked me why I hadn't come in the proper way, from Ockenford. 'A bird sanctuary is not an aviary,' I told him, 'Professor Agerbak particularly recommended that I approach from the estuary. He is our leading authority on the British waders.'

"I saw them eying each other and then they twitched their heads and I guessed I'd passed. 'O.K.,' they said, 'but mind you keep away from the area over to the right. Otherwise you'll find yourself in trouble.'

"I made a palaver about consulting my map. 'Would that be this blank space here?' I inquired innocently.

"One of them craned over and squinted at where I

was pointing. 'Yeah, that's it,' he said. 'There's a fence around it.'

" 'Not electrified, I hope.'

" 'What's that to you?'

" 'The *birds!*' I cried in a shocked voice. 'They can't *read,* you know!'

"They just laughed at that, revved up their engine and swooshed off, showering me with about a gallon of foul-smelling goo.

"I got the Skeeto started again and chugged on up the ditch, wondering what to do next. At least I'd learned that Benoit had been on the level as far as the location went and I thought I was beginning to see why he hadn't been able to pursue the matter any further. If the rest of the M.I.S. watchdogs were as sharp as those two, no one was going to get within half a mile of the place without being spotted. Then, just when I needed it most, I had a stroke of luck. I puttered around a bend in the creek and there, about a quarter of a mile ahead of me, I saw a low watchtower. At first I thought it must be something to do with the M.I.S., but as I got closer I saw it had a notice fixed to it saying it was the property of the R.O.S. There was even a metal landing stage. In a couple of shakes I'd tied up the Skeeto and shinned up the ladder.

"All it amounted to, really, was a wooden platform with low sides and a roof of thatched reeds, but for my purposes it was ideal. Up till then I'd hardly been able to see anything except the banks of the creek and one or two odd poles sticking up here and there, but now I had a clear view right out across the whole marsh. It's so flat down there that once you get up a few feet above reed level you can see for miles, and the first thing *I* saw was a flag fluttering from a flagpole on the roof of a long, black building about three-quarters of a mile north east of where I was lying. I got the glasses on to it and there was the old mailed fist flapping away

119

in the breeze, so at least there couldn't be any question about who was running the show.

"Then I started sweeping the area systematically. Those gorillas weren't joking about the fence! It's stranded wire strung from ten foot high concrete posts, and each post carries about a dozen evil looking insulators. There are a couple of gates with what look like guard houses beside them, and seven or eight smaller buildings scattered around. Leading to the north gate there's a concrete causeway which seems to come in from the direction of Ockenford. The other gate looks as if it opens straight on to another creek— I suppose that's where the hovercar came from.

"The really weird thing is that the whole place seems completely deserted. I must have been staring at it through the glasses for a good ten minutes before I saw someone. A bloke in black overalls came out of the main building, walked over to one of the others and disappeared inside. He's still in there for all I know! Then I tried concentrating on the main building. It's on two floors and there's a sort of penthouse affair on one end of the roof. What with that flag and the rows of dark windows the whole affair looks about as matey as a battleship. It occurred to me there must be some odd sort of glass in the windows because there was no reflection at all and yet I couldn't make out a damned thing on the inside. The only ordinary windows were in the penthouse and they had gray strip-blinds pulled down behind them.

"At about three the tide started coming in pretty fast and I had to scamble down and re-adjust the mooring rope on the Skeeto. At that point I was in two minds whether to pack up and go home—I was beginning to feel pretty tired and hungry—but I decided I might as well take one last peek. I'd no sooner crawled back up the ladder than I caught sight of something twinkling away off down the causeway. I got the glasses on to it and saw it was a land boat—jet black and about twice as long as Benoit's. It must have been doing close on a hundred because in a couple of minutes it was right up to the gates. They swung open and it rolled into the compound and came to a stop outside the main entrance to the battleship. The driver got out, scuttled around to the back, yanked open the rear door and saluted.

"The car was between me and them so I couldn't see the passenger getting out but as he straightened up he touched his cap to the driver and then turned toward me. For a couple of seconds I could have sworn he was staring straight at me—not at the tower, but at *me!* I know it was impossible—I was well out of eyesight range—but that didn't stop me ducking down and burying my face in the birdshit. When I looked up again he'd disappeared inside and the car was moving off."

"What was he like?" asked Carol.

"Quite old. In his sixties, I'd guess. Grey hair brushed back over his ears. A lot of lines on his face— two deep ones running down from the sides of his nose to the corners of his mouth. Clean shaven. Mouth about as friendly as a razor blade. He was tall too—at least six foot—and pretty lean with it. I suppose you could say he looked distinguished—the Cassius-type. You know—'*Yond Cassius has a lean and hungry look. Such men are dangerous*'."

"You don't know it was him, Laurie."

"It was him all right. We recognized one another."

"You *what?*"

"I can't explain it," he said, "but, somehow, when he turned and looked at me it was as if there was a sort of invisible thread stretched between us. Carol, I swear if that character wasn't Magobion then I don't exist."

"All right," she said. "Assuming it *was* him. Now what?"

Laurie nodded. "That's just what I've been asking myself for the last three hours," he admitted. "As far as I'm any judge there isn't a snowball in hell's chance that I could get inside the place without being picked up by the gorillas or fried on the wire. What's more I suspect that if it *could* have been done Benoit's boys would have done it months ago. No, the only way in there is straight up the causeway and through the front gate."

"And then?"

He shrugged. "You tell me."

"All right," she said, "I will. But you won't like it."

"Eh?" he muttered, relinquishing his own thoughts. "What won't I like?"

"What I'm going to say."

He blinked.

Noting the strain lines around his eyes and the stubborn downward turn of his lips, Carol felt a sudden welling-up of affection for him, something quite new and vulnerable and wholly human. She stretched out her hand across the table and touched his. "Drop it, Laurie," she said. "It's not for you, this one. Can't you see they're just using you? Manders and Benoit. To them you're just a convenient tool. Let them do their own dirty work. You've done more than enough. Far more."

Laurie looked simply baffled, as though she had suddenly started talking to him in a language he didn't understand. "Benoit?" he said. "What's Benoit got to do with it?"

"Well, Manders then," she continued desperately. "Don't you *see*, Laurie, this isn't really a NARCOS thing at all? All right, it might have seemed like one to start with, but now it's become something else again. You can't take on the whole of the M.I.S. single-handed! It's just crazy! Look, why don't you ring up Manders now? Tell him everything you've found out—

about Strübe and the rest of it—and then call it a day. Tomorrow we can both go off somewhere. Hells bells, I *am* on holiday, remember! Go on, Laurie. Do it. *Please.*"

To her surprise he nodded thoughtfully. "I was going to contact Manders anyway. It occurred to me that his brother might be able to help in some way."

"Well, go on then," she urged. "Do it now. I'll make us some coffee."

He pushed back his chair, thrust himself up from the table and walked slowly through into the other room.

Carol expelled her breath in a long-drawn-out sigh, gathered up the dishes and slotted them into the autorinse. Then she filled the electric coffee volcano and switched it on. She had just finished clearing the table and the volcano was starting to erupt when Laurie reappeared.

"That didn't take long," she said. "Wasn't he in?"

He looked at her and then at the snorting coffee cone and it seemed to Carol that he was still listening to some voice inside his own head.

"Well?" she nudged him. "What happened?"

He sat down heavily and laid his hands palm flat on the table before him. "Manders is dead," he said.

For a second or two the only sound in the tiny room came from the splurting machine. Carol and Laurie simply stared at each other. Then he said: "On Sunday. Sunday night."

"But *how?*" she whispered. "What happened?"

"They say he shot himself."

"Oh, *Laurie!* No!"

"I can't believe it either," he said. "He was killed, Caro. I'm sure of it. They must have killed him because they couldn't shut him up."

"The report on Lynn . . . ?"

"What else? He would have sent it off the day after

123

we had supper with him. He *must* have known what
he was doing."

"Oh Jesus!" she whispered. "That must have been
what they were looking for here! The copy we took to
Martell!"

"It looks like it, doesn't it?"

"I feel sick, Laurie."

"The poor old devil," he muttered. "He really *was* a
good man, Caro. He deserved something better than
that."

"What are you going to do?" she asked fearfully.

He just looked at her.

"They'll kill you too, Laurie!"

He shrugged. "Like the man said—*We all owe God
a death.*"

It was then that she knew with absolute certainty
that nothing she could say would divert him from his
purpose. She might argue with him till words lost their
meaning and it would be as if she had never spoken at
all. And she knew too that Manders' death was only
an incidental spur to his intention, the final franking
on a letter that had long since been written and
stamped and addressed. For a flickering moment she
seemed to be standing outside herself as though she
were a spectator at a play that she had seen played
through before but whose final act, even so, she could
not quite remember. In a world of shadows she too
had become a shadow. And then the moment passed
and she knew only that she was afraid again, afraid for
him, and for herself, and even, a little, for the world.

Major Gross was watching the ten o'clock So-V
newscast when his wife came into the room and told
him that two young NARCOS agents were asking for
him.

"At this hour?" he protested. "What do they want?"

"They wouldn't tell me, dear. But they insist it's extremely urgent."

"Oh, very well. Show them in," he grumbled and regretfully relinquished the processed atrocities of the war in South Africa.

He recognized Laurie's voice before he saw him. "Hel-*lo*, Linton!" he called. "What brings you here at this hour?"

"I'm sorry I couldn't let you know, sir, but we suspected our phone was being tapped. This is 3rd Officer Kennedy—Carol. She's with London Records."

"Delighted to meet you, Miss Kennedy. Let me get you both something to drink. While I'm doing it you sit yourselves down and tell me what this is all about."

Laurie took a deep breath. "I'm not sure how much you already know, sir."

" 'Know'?" repeated Major Gross vaguely. "About what precisely?"

"Well, do you know that Doctor Manders is dead?"

"Good God!"

"He's supposed to have committed suicide."

"Jimmy *Manders! Kill* himself? Poppycock!"

"I know," said Laurie.

"When did this happen?"

"On Sunday night apparently. I only heard about it this evening when I tried to contact him at the Center. They told me he'd shot himself."

Major Gross shook his head. "Go on," he growled ominously.

Laurie glanced at Carol. "I suppose he must have told you what I was doing for him, sir?"

"He was not particularly explicit," said Gross guardedly. "We agreed it was probably better to leave it that way. But this. . . ."

"Sir. Can you tell me who had me taken off the inquiry?"

"Jimmy told you that, did he?"

Laurie nodded. "I must know, sir. It's vital."

Major Gross pursed up his lips and regarded the two of them thoughtfully. "As a matter of fact it was a Home Office directive."

"*Home Office!* Not the M.I.S.?"

Gross frowned. "Look here, Linton," he said, "it strikes me you'd better go right back to the beginning and tell me everything. It could well be that you're swimming out into some pretty deep water."

He handed them each a glass of sherry and took one for himself. "From the beginning," he said. "And if you've no objections I'll tape it."

So Laurie recounted, more or less chronologically, all that had happened to him since he had first been assigned to the Director of the Rehabilitation Center. He even described his encounter with Lynn. He did not, however, speak about what had happened to him in 1987, or about Carol's dream.

When it was finished Major Gross sat staring into space. "Piers Magobion," he murmured. "Yes, that tallies."

"You know him, sir?"

Gross nodded. "A politico," he said. "Damned clever fellow. *Too* damned clever."

"Then he's not an army colonel?"

"Oh, yes, he's that all right, and a hell of a lot else besides."

"What *is* his role in the M.I.S., sir?"

"I'm not exactly sure," said Cross. "There are plenty of rumors, of course."

"What sort of rumors?"

"That he calls the tune for **Darley, for one.**"

"The Home Secretary?"

Gross nodded. "There were quite a few people who took a jaundiced view of things when the M.I.S. ab-

126

sorbed those M.O.D. departments. The point is, of course, that Magobion's been running them a damn sight more efficiently than they'd ever been run before."

"That was what Doctor Manders said about the Center."

Gross scratched his chin. "When you come to think of it, it's an odd sort of empire Magobion's tacked together. Not quite army; not quite police. Betwixt and between."

Laurie leaned forward. "I want to go down there, sir. To Gowers Marsh. I'm sure there's something going on we ought to know about."

"It's out of the question, Linton. You know we can't stick our necks out where National Security's involved. Look what happened in '93—and there we *did* have a case!"

"But this is different, sir. It's not just ordinary narcotics, it's—"

"Precisely! I'm sorry, Linton. That one's just not on. The risk's far too great."

Laurie stared down at the carpet and fought to master his anger and his disappointment. "And Doctor Manders?" he said bitterly. "What about *him?*"

"I don't follow you."

"He was killed," said Laurie. "Have you forgotten?"

"I only have your word—" Gross began to bluster and then caught the gleam of cold contempt in Laurie's eye. "Well, that's a matter for the police."

"You know they won't do anything. Why should they? They closed their file on Lynn without batting an eyelid."

Major Gross got up from his chair and began pacing up and down the room. "Besides," he muttered, "even if you did go down there, what could you possibly hope to achieve? Just supposing you even managed to set foot in the place, they'd make pretty damned sure you

127

never saw anything they didn't want you to see. These people aren't amateurs, you know."

"Nor are we, sir. I'm not asking for a U.N.O. search warrant. I just want to get a look at the place from the inside."

"And just what sort of excuse had you thought of giving for that?" demanded the Major ironically.

"The Benoit connection."

Gross halted in his tracks and stared at Laurie. "The Benoit connection?" he murmured. "You know that's not bad, Linton. Not bad at all."

Laurie seized his chance. "All we've got to say, sir, is that we suspect large consignments are being off-loaded in the marsh from foreign ships coming into Tilbury. We can make out we're anxious to question their gorillas—find out if they've noticed anything unusual going on. As a cover-up it's virtually fool-proof. The more open we are the less they'll be able to refuse. After all, they're supposed to be on our side, aren't they?"

"On our side?"

" 'All member governments hereby undertake to co-operate to the full in eradicating the menace of narcotics trafficking'," Laurie rattled off glibly.

Major Gross gave a mirthless snort. "Look here," he said. "Just supposing I was prepared to give you a green on this one—and I'm not saying I will, for one moment—what would you want?"

"A car and a gun," said Laurie promptly.

"A gun?"

Laurie looked him squarely in the eye. "In case I feel inspired to blow out my brains—like Doctor Manders."

The shot went home. But though Gross knew that Laurie was perfectly capable of handling firearms he was obviously unhappy at the idea. "Well, Miss Kennedy?" he said, turning to Carol, who had been sitting

128

almost entirely mute throughout the interview. "And what's your opinion?"

The truth was that Carol didn't know what her opinion was, but she guessed there might be slightly less of a risk if Laurie went in with her under the NARCOS banner than if he attempted to go in alone under none. "If we go there's just a chance we may learn something useful, sir. If we don't go we'll never learn anything."

Gross eyed her with a new respect. "You're aiming to be in on this too, are you?"

"Two pairs of eyes are better than one," said Laurie. "Especially in this sort of open-ended operation."

Gross nodded, pondered for some seconds, then walked purposefully over to a writing desk in a corner of the room. "All right, Linton," he said, "you can have a go. I won't pretend I'm enthusiastic because I'm not. As far as NARCOS is concerned, this investigation is a totally new assignment, quite separate from anything you may have been doing for Doctor Manders." He scribbled something on a pad, ripped off the sheet and handed it to Laurie. "One Semling automatic authorized to you personally, Linton, for twenty-four hours, commencing at 0900 tomorrow. You can pick up a car at the same time. I suppose you'd both better stay in the hostel for tonight." He lifted the receiver of the video-phone and cocked an eyebrow at Carol. "One room or two, Miss Kennedy?"

"One," she said.

"Lucky Linton."

As they were leaving, Laurie turned to the Major. "I know it's none of my business, sir," he said, "but you knew Doctor Manders pretty well, didn't you?"

"Yes," admitted Gross. "I think you could say that."

"You don't think he *did* kill himself, do you?"

"I'm damned sure he didn't! What's more, if I

thought he *had* you don't suppose I'd be underwriting this little carry-on, do you?"

"No," said Laurie. "That's really why I asked."

The grizzled Master Sergeant in charge of the Dachet Armory tightened the buckles of the filigree webbing around Laurie's ribs and handed him back his uniform jacket. Laurie shrugged it on, fastened the buttons and eyed himself critically in the mirror.

"Right, sir," said the Sergeant, pointing toward the butts. "Now let's have six rapid in Number 3."

Laurie drew a deep breath, walked forward and eyed the target. Then he loosened the top button and nodded.

"Fahr!" yelled the Sergeant.

In one smooth movement Laurie had crouched, his right hand had leaped to his breast and the slender black automatic was bucking between his hands. He straightened up and inhaled the deadly breath of gunsmoke as he watched the colored score-lights register two vitals, two hits, and two misses.

The Sergeant sniffed disparagingly. "In *twos*, Mr. Linton," he growled. "That's not a bloody machine-gun you've got there! Try another six."

Laurie removed the spent clip, fed in another, and reholstered one gun.

"Number 4," said the Sergeant. "In your own time."

The results this time were distinctly better. The Sergeant nodded. "All right," he said. "You feel happy with that, do you, sir?"

Laurie agreed that he did.

"Six clips of ammo?"

"Thank you, Sergeant."

"The Semling's a nice little weapon," said the Sergeant, writing some figures on a pad and pushing it across the counter for Laurie to sign. "Never known one to jam up. Still, let's hope you won't need to use it, eh?"

Laurie smiled and signed his name on the bottom of the authorization sheet. "Have you ever killed anyone, Sergeant?"

"Not since Belfast '72. Takes us back a bit, doesn't it?"

Laurie handed back the pad and the pen. The Sergeant slid the clips of ammunition across the counter. Laurie picked one up, glanced at it and thrust it into the gun. The others went into his pockets. "Tell me, Sergeant," he said. "What did it feel like?"

The Sergeant shrugged. "I don't know as I felt anything very much, Mr. Linton. It was them or us, see?"

"Them or us," murmured Laurie. "Yes, I suppose it would have been." He smiled at the leathery face before him. "Well, thank you, Sergeant. I'll bring it back to you tomorrow."

The Sergeant grinned. "You'd better, sir, or we'll both be in the doghouse. Good luck."

He watched as Laurie walked away down the concrete passage. "The trouble with you, Mr. Linton," he muttered to himself, "is that you think too bloody much."

Carol was waiting beside the car in the transport bay. Like Laurie she had donned uniform for the trip to Dachet—dark blue with the silver, lightning bolt insignia on the lapels of the jacket. As she watched him walking toward her with his head slightly bent against the fine drizzling rain, she was assailed once again with the overwhelming conviction that this had all happened before. It was as though while someone else was turning the pages of a photograph album she had glimpsed a print which seemed to be familiar, but now she was unable to find it again.

Laurie glanced up, caught sight of her and grinned. "Did you remember the Urban Registration?"

131

"What do you suppose that is?" she retorted, indicating the sticker on the windscreen.

"Then we're all set?"

Carol nodded. "How long will it take us to get there?"

"About an hour and a half. Maybe less. It depends on the arterials. We can take the M501 almost as far as Ockenford." He opened the car and glanced inside. "I must say I preferred the Koyota on the whole. Still, no doubt this is more in keeping with the official image. O.K. In you get."

They belted themselves in and Laurie set the mileometer. Just as he was about to twist the ignition key he turned to Carol. "Scared?"

"Not scared," she corrected. "Just plain terrified."

"You don't *have* to come, Caro. You know that."

"Oh, for Christ's sake!" she exploded. "Get on with it, will you, or I'll have to go and pee again!"

Laurie laughed and flicked the engine into life.

They made excellent time into London. The car— one of the standard NARCOS Fords—had been serviced and tuned only two days before and it positively relished the chance to show what it could do. Furthermore the stenciled insignia on the doors gave them virtual immunity from the Highway Patrols. They zoomed around the Hammersmith intersection and reached the Dagenham control barrier exactly forty-five minutes after leaving Dachet. Fifteen minutes later they filtered off the M501 and headed for Ockenford.

The drizzle which had held off during the earlier part of the drive now began to fall again. The sky resembled gray porridge and the marshes beneath it had a look of forlorn desolation that did nothing to lift the spirits. They stopped in Ockenford and inquired the way to the Department of Psychological Strategy.

The woman they asked looked at them blankly and confessed that she had never heard of it.

"It's in the bird sanctuary," said Laurie. "A big black building with a fence round it."

"Oh, you mean the *'orspital!*" she cried. "Go on down this road for 'alf a mile and you'll see a gray gate on your right—you can't miss it. 'S a private road, see? The 'orspital's about a coupler miles on down there."

They thanked her and drove on. "Hospital?" said Carol. "I don't much care for the sound of that."

To their surprise the gray gate was standing open. A large notice board beside it informed them unequivocally that they were entering Government Property and that no unauthorized person was permitted to set foot therein. Before them like a combed parting the concrete causeway rolled drearily away between the ranks of dun-colored reeds and, right at its end, they could just make out the roof of the penthouse and the tiny smudge of the limp flag.

Laurie reached over into the seat behind him, retrieved his uniform cap and settled it firmly on his head. "Every little bit helps," he said. "How do I look?"

"Vulnerable," said Carol.

"But official with it, I hope."

She smiled wanly. "Oh yes. Highly official."

"Well, death or glory then," he said and let in the clutch.

In the M.I.S. guardhouse the NARCOS car had been picked up on the monitor screens the moment it approached the outer gate, and it remained under surveillance throughout its passage down the causeway. As it neared the compound the guard requested instructions and was told to admit it. In consequence, as Laurie was about to draw up in front of the gates, they

133

swung inward. "Well, well," he murmured. "What price the walls of Jericho?"

They rolled forward and pulled up beside the guardhouse. As they did so the gates closed quietly behind them. Carol shivered and felt as though ice-cold knuckles were kneading her stomach. Laurie released his safety web and clambered out. "Hang on," he said loudly. "I'll go and have a word with whoever's in charge here."

As he strode briskly up to the guardroom door it was opened from within and a man in black uniform appeared on the threshold. "Can I help you?" he inquired civilly.

"Are you in charge here?" asked Laurie in his best pukkah accent.

The man eyed him curiously. "That depends, sir," he said. "What was it you were wanting?"

"I'm afraid that has to come under the heading of Classified Information," said Laurie. "It's to do with a line of inquiry we're following up for NARCOS. I'd be happy to explain to your Commanding Officer."

"But of course, Mr. Linton," said a suave voice from the guardhouse.

Laurie stared over the guard's shoulder and realized, sickly, that the voice was coming from a speaker just inside the doorway.

"Sergeant Rogers will show you the way," continued the voice. "And do bring Miss Kennedy with you."

Before Laurie was able to frame an adequate reply the voice spoke again. "There is just one formality, Mr. Linton. Would you be so good as to leave your weapon in the guardhouse? It will be returned to you when you leave."

Laurie blinked at the impassive guard. "Weapon?" he said vaguely.

There was a discreet cough from the speaker. "The gun in the pectoral holster, Mr. Linton."

Laurie shrugged sheepishly, slid his hand into his breast and produced the automatic. The guard took it, glanced at it and nodded.

"Thank you, Mr. Linton. A pure formality, you understand. Carry on, Rogers."

The guard disappeared into the guardhouse and Laurie walked slowly back toward the car. "You heard that?" he whispered.

Carol rolled her eyes. "Do you want to know how I feel?" she muttered.

"They wouldn't dare try anything, Caro."

"Try telling that to Manders," she retorted, and climbed out of the car as the guard reappeared and asked them to follow him.

They paced along the metaled roadway down which Laurie had seen the black land-boat roll the previous afternoon. There was no sign of it now. Soft as fleece the misty drizzle wafted in over the marsh and beaded damply along their eyelashes. The guard's plastic-soled boots left a pattern of dark bars on the shiny asphalt. Laurie felt the numb sense of fatality that the condemned prisoner must feel on his last walk to the scaffold, and yet, along with it, was an unmistakable and quickening curiosity whose roots lay far back in his past in an overgrown gulley beside a brawling mountain river. What unknown threads had been spun to weave the mysterious net in which they were now entangled? Which came first, the spinner or the web?

Approaching the long black building Laurie glanced up and saw a figure standing at the penthouse window gazing down at them. Some strange whim prompted him to raise his hand to his cap in ironic salute, and he was not in the least surprised to see the watcher twitch his own hand in a token gesture of acknowledgment.

As they ascended the steps which led up to the main

door the NARCOS agent within Laurie reasserted himself. It was within these walls, if anywhere, that the extraordinary properties of *Kállos-12* were being explored, mapped, and, presumably, exploited. But on entering the building, he found himself directed on to a spiral flow-way by the impassive Sergeant Rogers. Access to the ground floor was barred from prying eyes by two doors of that same dark material which, Laurie guessed, had been used to glaze the outer windows.

Rogers set the flow-way in motion and they corkscrewed silently upward past the landing of the second floor which appeared identical in every respect with the one below it. Not once did they catch so much as a glimpse of another human being or hear the sound of any other voice.

They were finally deposited at the end of a short, covered passageway, paved with black rubber and roofed with translucent tiles. The Sergeant proceeded along it at the same stately pace he had employed ever since they had left the guardhouse, and placed his hand, palm-flat on a sensitized lock-plate in the wall. The door at the end of the passage slid open silently. "Mr. Linton and Miss Kennedy, sir," he announced.

"Thank you, Rogers," said the same voice that had addressed Laurie from the guardhouse. "Show them in."

Sergeant Rogers stood to one side and beckoned to Laurie and Carol with a jerk of his head. They exchanged a brief questioning glance and then walked forward into the carpeted ante-room beyond. As Laurie moved past him the Sergeant breathed the one word, "Cap!" into his ear. Laurie shrugged, pulled off his cap, and tucked it under his arm.

They crossed the book-lined ante-room and emerged into the penthouse proper—a wide, comfortably furnished room with windows on three sides. The fourth wall, through which they had entered, supported a battery of at least a dozen monitor screens and a built-in console. A large desk was aligned in front of it.

"Welcome to my eyrie!" The tall, uniformed figure turned away from the window where he had been standing. "Do I need to introduce myself?"

"Colonel Magobion?"

"Yes, Mr. Linton, I am Colonel Magobion." From beneath bristling gray brows a pair of the bluest eyes Laurie had ever seen surveyed him throughly before moving on to Carol. "Miss Kennedy."

"How do you know my name?" asked Carol.

The Colonel smiled. "I lay no claim to omniscience, Miss Kennedy. Nevertheless our Imbuishi Ovonic Cortex is exhaustively programed and would, I daresay, make the I.V.K. digital at your Records Office look somewhat primitive. But do, please, sit down. Isn't this a remarkable view? Even on a day like this I find it has a mysterious and melancholy attraction. Do either of you ever read Edgar Allan Poe? No? Then, alas, you will not appreciate my reference to *The Fall of the House of Usher.*" He sighed, clasped his hands behind his back, and hunched his shoulders like a brooding eagle. "Well now, Mr. Linton, you mentioned to Sergeant Rogers a particular line of investigation you are pursuing. May I be allowed to know what it is?"

Laurie stared at him. Having convinced himself that Magobion was totally in control of the situation, he assumed that the old man must be deriving some sick sort of satisfaction from playing cat-and-mouse with them. He was on the point of throwing in his hand and confessing the real reason for their being there when some deep-seated instinct for self-preservation made him pause. If this was the way Magobion wanted it, why not humor him? So he fiexed the old man with a frank and steadfast gaze and produced the cover-story that he and Carol had cooked up the night before.

As he warmed to his task he found the spurious circumstantial details rising like bubbles in his imagination. Had not the blue and white Skeeto that Angie had seen abducting Jim been observed several times in the region of Carling's Creek? Had not the Swiss connection been established and confirmed? Was there not a singularly reliable underworld tip-off that a major consignment of heroin was due in sometime this week? Was it not possible that some of the Colonel's guards had observed suspicious activity in the marshes? And as for the reason he had not felt able to speak of this to Sergeant Rogers? Why, simply that there was still an outside chance that someone *actually within this establishment* might prove to be actively involved. By the time he had finished Laurie was more than half way to believing his own lies and Carol was regarding him with unfeigned admiration.

As Magobion stared down at him Laurie felt the first faint sparks of renewed hope beginning to glow among the dead ashes. Was it, after all, possible that the Colonel's knowledge was less than total? What *had* he known about them apart from their names and the fact that one of them was carrying a gun, and a simple X-ray monitor probe would have shown him that? Laurie raced back frantically through the events of the past ten minutes and could discover nothing more substantial than their own fears. He smiled blandly. "So you will understand, sir, that we would very much appreciate any help you could give us in this matter."

Magobion nodded. "This Swiss connection," he said. "Can you give me any more details?"

"There's certainly a very big operator involved,"

said Laurie. "We know a good deal about him, but so far we haven't been able to pin anything on to him. The bigger they come, the slipperier they get."

"What is his name?"

Laurie pursed up his lips and glanced across at Carol—a portrayal of a troubled conscience worthy of any So-Vi Oscar. Finally he shook his head. "You put me in a very awkward situation, sir. Until we've actually got him in the bag we're bound to talk of him as 'Mr. X.' It's different with the smaller fry but he's a big fish."

"Would it, by any chance, be a certain Gabriel Benoit?"

Laurie's look of startled surprise was perfect. "You *know?*" he gasped.

It was Magobion's turn to look smug. "NARCOS are not the only people who are interested in the activities of Gabriel Benoit, Mr. Linton."

Laurie's sole fear at that moment was that he would be unable to conceal his exultation. He dearly wished he could get Carol away into some quiet corner, free of monitor eyes and eavesdroppers, and there bask in her adulation. He leaned forward eagerly. "Would you care to be a little more explicit, sir?"

Magobion shrugged. "It's an involved story," he said vaguely. "A couple of years ago *Mondiale* loaned one of their chaps to us for a particular project I was in charge of. As you're probably aware, Benoit carries considerable weight in *Mondiale*. In fact, in one way or another he's caused us quite a bit of trouble." He smiled thinly. "Frankly, Mr. Linton, I don't suppose I'd shed a single tear if that gentleman were to find himself in Queer Street."

Laurie clicked his fingers. "Just a moment," he said. "This rings a bell somewhere." He half-closed his eyes and frowned in a parody of concentration. "Strübe? Karl Strübe?"

"You know about Strübe?" Magobion's tone was mildly curious, nothing more.

"It was common gossip at *Mondiale*," said Laurie. "Isn't the case still under consideration at The Hague?"

"You're remarkably well informed, Mr. Linton."

Laurie shrugged modestly. "Oh, we're trained to keep our ears open in NARCOS, Colonel. You'd be surprised at the sort of thing one hears."

"Then surprise me, Mr. Linton."

"Well, I don't remember all the ins and outs of that Strübe business—something to do with research into neuronal enzymes, wasn't it? It's not my field at all, but Doctor Dring was pretty excited about it."

"Indeed? And who is Doctor Dring?"

"He's a colleague of Benoit's. Works for *Mondiale* in Geneva."

"And when did Doctor Dring tell you this?"

"A few days ago."

Carol frowned. "I don't see what this has to do with our present case," she said. "Hadn't you better ask the Colonel if we can question his staff?"

"You're right," said Laurie. "If we *are* ever to put Benoit in Queer Street, now's our chance. What do you think our best line would be, Colonel?"

Magobion turned away and walked to the window. "Your best line, Mr. Linton?" he repeated. "Ah, now, I wonder which that would be?"

"What I'd really appreciate would be a chance to chat informally to some of your men, sir."

Magobion had his back to them. "I'm sure you would, Mr. Linton," he murmured, "but I regret that will not be possible." He rocked slowly on his heels and toes and gazed out across the weeping estuary.

"Oh," said Laurie. "Well, in that case, sir, perhaps you have some other suggestion."

Magobion's hands were clasped across the small of

his back, the right one alternately gripping and re-leasing the left. "You place me in a very awkward situation," he murmured. "Very awkward indeed."

Laurie pulled a doubtful face at Carol who, for her part, looked pale and apprehensive. "Of course, sir, you must realize that I'm not suggesting that any of your staff are anything but completely . . ."

Magobion contrived to ignore this interruption almost as if he were genuinely unaware of it. "Had you stopped even at Strübe," he murmured, "I should probably have overlooked it. After all, as you yourself pointed out, Strübe's case did create something of a stir in *Mondiale*. But then you made the fatal error of specifying neuronal enzymes. You see, Mr. Linton, nobody in the world, apart from myself, knows that Karl Strübe was ever engaged on the synthesis of neuronal enzymes. *Not even Strübe himself!*" He turned and fixed Laurie with a cold, accusing stare. "So how did *you* discover it, Mr. Linton?"

Laurie felt as though cold and clammy hands were crawling all over his naked body. "But I've already told you, Colonel! It was Doctor Dring who—"

"You were lying."

"Oh, but this is ridiculous!" Laurie protested. "What the hell do I care what Strübe was working on? Benoit's the one I'm after."

"Who sent you here?"

"Nobody sent us. It was the obvious step to—"

"Was it Benoit?"

"*Benoit!* Good God, sir, you can't seriously think that I'd—"

"I have to *know*, Mr. Linton. I need hardly remind you that I have the necessary means at my disposal to elicit this information. Furthermore, you have effectively placed yourself under my jurisdiction. Come now, the time for prevarication is over."

Laurie knew this was no bluff. Whatever advantage he might previously have gained he had thrown away in his drunken euphoria. He glanced past Magobion, out across the deserted compound to the fence where, by unhappy chance, his eye alighted on the charred remnants of some unidentifiable sea-bird. "Nobody sent us here," he said, "and that's the truth. It was my own idea entirely."

"I am afraid I find that quite impossible to believe, Mr. Linton."

"I wonder why?" said Laurie. "It seems straightforward enough to me."

"We know you were working for Doctor Manders."

"On the contrary, I was working for NARCOS. I still am."

"We know Manders showed you a report he had prepared on one of his cases—the girl he called 'Catherine'."

Laurie shrugged. "So?"

"Where is that report now, Mr. Linton?"

"Why don't you ask Manders? It's his report."

"We did. He told us he'd given a copy to you."

"That's riduculous!"

"We have the best of reasons for knowing that he was not lying. *Where is that copy, Mr. Linton?*"

Again Laurie shrugged. "All right," he said. "If you must know, it was stolen."

"*Stolen!*" For the first time Magobion sounded genuinely startled.

Laurie nodded. "Doctor Manders asked me to pass it on to Dring in Geneva. While we were out our hotel room was ransacked and the report was taken. That's the last I ever saw of it."

"When did this happen?"

"Monday evening, wasn't it, Caro?"

Carol nodded. "They bugged our room at the same time."

" 'They'?"

142

"Whoever did it," she said.

"You don't know who it was?"

"We assumed it was Benoit."

"Why Benoit?"

"I think he suspected we had a line on him," said Laurie. "We'd found out that a cat called Nadler was busy in London and we knew that Nadler had done jobs for Benoit in the past. What we couldn't fathom was why Benoit should want the report at all. Our guess was that whoever took it thought it was something else. Anyway, I can't see what all the fuss is about. It was only a copy after all."

"In the wrong hands, Mr. Linton, even that copy could prove extremely dangerous."

"Dangerous? Who to?"

"The security of this nation."

"Oh, come off it!" said Laurie.

"We happen to know that Benoit has political connections with the Asiatic bloc."

"And what's that supposed to prove? He has connections all over the place."

"How much did he offer you, Mr. Linton?"

Laurie gulped. "If that's meant to be a joke, then all I can say is it's in bloody poor taste!"

Magobion surveyed him coldly. "You almost persuade me that you have integrity," he murmured. "Very well, I admit I have no proof that you are in the pay of Benoit. Now will you be so good as to tell me how you came to learn that Doctor Strübe was working on neuronal enzymes?"

Laurie spread his hands. "But I *have* told you," he said. "Doctor Dring said so. He asked me if I had read Manders' report. I told him as much as I could remember—which wasn't much incidentally—and he said it looked as though someone had succeeded in synthesizing one of the neuronal enzymes. That's when he told me he'd heard that Strübe had been working on them. For all I know it could have been just an inspired guess on his part. As for me I wouldn't recognize a neuronal enzyme if you showed me one."

Magobion moved slowly back to his station by the window. For a while he simply stood there, staring out toward the distant estuary. Finally he said: "I think it is possible—*just* possible—that you are telling the truth. If I were free to do so I believe I might even be prepared to overlook what has occurred. However, I am not in that position. You already know too much for your own safety. Consequently you leave me with no alternative but to ensure that you do not communicate that knowledge to other people."

Laurie's reaction was an incredulous laugh. "But everything we've told you has already been recorded!"

"Why must you persist in underestimating me, Mr. Linton? Before you leave here you will have told me everything you know. Everything. Nor do I anticipate that your superiors will prove unduly obstructive, since you will both deny all knowledge of this particular episode, even to the extent of reporting that you failed to gain admission."

"Now just a minute," muttered Laurie, rising to his feet. "You aren't thinking of playing any of your Strübe games with us, are you Colonel?"

"I do not play games, Mr. Linton. As I said before you have placed yourselves voluntarily under my jurisdiction. In the interests of National Security it is imperative that you forget this interview has ever taken place."

He had taken two steps toward the side of the room which held the monitor screens when Laurie moved sideways and blocked his path. "Not so fast, Colonel," he murmured. "Caro, run and see if you can't fix that door."

Magobion's blue eyes blazed angrily. "Stand aside, Mr. Linton!"

144

"All in good time, Colonel. I want you to understand that we have every intention of leaving here with our memories intact—even if it means taking you along with us. Now why don't you just sit down quietly and tell us what it is you're so afraid anyone will find out?"

Magobion measured the distance to the control panel with his eye but Laurie shook his head warningly. "Don't try it, Colonel. I'd hate to have to chop down an old man."

"You realize, of course, that you are condemning yourselves to death."

"Is that what Manders did?" Without warning Laurie grabbed the Colonel by the arms, swung him off-balance, and thrust him down into an arm chair.

Carol came back into the room. "I think I've done it," she said.

"Pass me that paper knife, Caro."

She picked up a long sliver of polished obsidian from the desk and handed it to him.

Without taking his eyes off the old man, Laurie tested the needle-sharp point against his spread palm. "While you were out, Caro, the Colonel decided to review his sentence on us. We've now been condemned to death. What do you think of that?"

Carol's lips tightened. She shook her head.

"Well, I think it was poor psychology," said Laurie, "because we now have nothing left to lose." He moved around behind the Colonel's chair, leaned forward and touched the point of the knife against the soft flesh below the old man's right ear. "So tell us what you're up to, you murderous old rogue," he murmured, "or I swear to God I'll shove this right up into your scheming brain." And to show that he meant what he said he prodded the point home.

Magobion's face turned a sickly gray. A single dark

bead of blood rose glistening upon the punctured skin. "This is treason," he whispered.

"I wondered if it might be," said Laurie. "So go ahead and tell us. We'll start with K-12. What does it do?"

"Who *are* you?"

"Don't change the subject, Colonel. Time's precious." And to emphasize his words Laurie gave the mottled flesh another painful prick. "What does K-12 do?"

"It releases psychokinetic energy," gasped the old man and it was as though the words were being drawn out of him with pincers.

"Go on."

"It has enabled us to marshal those energies and to control them."

"And what do you hope to achieve by that?"

This question produced an extraordinary metamorphosis in Magobion's expression. Impotent fury gave place to something almost akin to serenity. "Hope to achieve?" he repeated. "I can assure you it is no longer a hope. I have achieved it."

"Achieved *what*, for God's sake?"

Somehow the old man contrived to draw himself upright in the chair. He gazed out past Carol to some point that only he could see. "The ultimate," he murmured. "I have achieved the ultimate. At this very moment I effectively control the guidance system of every single orbital and ballistic missile in the Western hemisphere!"

Laurie felt the angel's wing caress of that wholly instinctive fear that grips the sane in the presence of insanity. "You're mad," he said. "No one can do that." And then he remembered Professor Martell.

Magobion did not deign to reply.

"Who else knows about this?"

Magobion remained silent.

"Speak up, man," growled Laurie. "The War Office? The Prime Minister? Who?"

The only response was a glance of withering contempt.

"Well, who's running this show?"

"My staff."

"Where are they then?"

No response.

Laurie's patience deserted him. He whipped the point of the stiletto around to the baggy flesh under the old man's chin and jerked it upward an agonizing quarter of an inch. "Where are they?" he repeated.

The aquiline head strained backward; the sinews in the scrawny neck drew taut as bowstrings. "You fool, boy," he whispered. "What can you know of power?"

"Then tell me," said Laurie and lowered the knife.

Magobion licked his dry lips. "Power," he said huskily, "true power, power such as I possess, *cannot be shared!* To delegate is to dilute. Direct control must be retained in the hands of *one single person.* That is the secret. Once the ultimate pinnacle has been reached, the ladder which enabled one to climb there must be dispensed with. All power is holy: absolute power is divine."

Laurie stared at him incredulously. "You really are insane."

"Rubbish, boy! I have simply achieved what every other autocrat has only dreamt about. Why, if you were honest with yourself you would have to admit that you are savoring every moment of this situation." He chuckled mirthlessly. "You know I can almost find it in myself to envy you."

"What can we do with him, Caro? Kill him?"

"We've still got to get out of here somehow."

"But without proof?" he said. "Who's ever going to believe us?"

147

They glanced at one another and then back at the Colonel. "We'll have to take him with us," she said.

Laurie nodded. "He knows what'll happen if he tries anything. You do, don't you Colonel?"

Magobion, who seemed to be recovering his self-possession with every passing second, inclined his head submissively.

"Go and unlock the door, Caro. Right, Colonel, up on your feet. But try anything on and they'll be blowing the *Last Post* over you. Got that?"

"You make yourself admirably plain, Mr. Linton."

"I hope so for your sake," said Laurie retrieving his cap and using it to conceal the knife. "Now lead the way."

They passed through the ante-room and down the passage to the flow-way. "We'll walk it," said Laurie. "Stop at the first landing, Colonel. You're giving us the conducted tour, remember. What's in here?"

"The incubator unit."

"What's that?"

"See for yourselves."

"All right. Open up."

Magobion walked up to the double doors and placed his hand on the sensitized plate. As the panels slid apart Laurie and Carol found themselves gazing into a long dark tunnel. On either side were ranged some twenty or thirty transparent capsule cells, each dimly lit by a ruby glow-lamp. The atmosphere within the tunnel was warm, stifling and oppressive.

"I'm afraid we must close the door behind us," said Magobion. "The light disturbs them."

"Be very careful, Colonel," Laurie warned him, prodding the muffled point into his back.

"Believe me I shall, Mr. Linton."

As the doors whispered shut and their eyes adapted to the roseate gloom Laurie and Carol saw that each cell contained the naked body of a dark-skinned, adolescent girl curled up in the foetal position on a transparent hydro-mattress. All the bodies were connected by flexible umbilicas to a stave of pipes which ran the length of the building and passed through the roof of each cell.

"But who are they?" whispered Carol.

"They are my dreamers," murmured Magobion, and, as he spoke, one half of each of the hydro-mattresses slowly swelled, rolling its sleeper gently over on to its other side. "Are they not beautiful, Miss Kennedy, my little devotees of *Kállos*? What unimaginable bliss is theirs? What exquisite nirvana? Can you conceive how cruelly distressed they will be when they learn that you intend to take it from them? See, the merest hint of such an enormity is sufficient to disturb them!" And, sure enough, as he spoke, the sleepers they were watching stirred restlessly, wherupon he began to murmur in some foreign tongue that neither Laurie nor Carol understood or even recognized.

"Shut up!" growled Laurie and made a wild grab for the old man's arm. Next moment he was tossed backward like a straw in a whirlwind, to crash with stunning force against the closed doors. Carol screamed in terror. The knife was whisked from Laurie's nerveless fingers and vanished in the crimson gloom. In a matter of seconds he had been rendered totally powerless.

From the shadows Magobion chuckled drily. "I told you they would be angry with you, Mr. Linton. Are you surprised?"

Laurie lunged forward only to find himself thrust back against the door, spreadeagled as though by some enormous, invisible hand. "I should have killed you while I had the chance," he groaned.

"You certainly will not have another," said Magobion. "I fully intend to give myself the pleasure of seeing you dismembered, Mr. Linton. They can do it, you know. Their concerted power really is utterly phenomenal. Which is strange when you consider that they themselves are such gentle, fragile creatures. Do you not agree?"

"Caro? Are you all right?"

"Miss Kennedy is being temporarily restrained," Magobion informed him. "If she behaves herself she will not be unduly harmed."

Out of the corner of his eye Laurie could just distinguish the darker square on the wall which he knew must be the sensitized plate operating the doors. He guessed that it would have been set to reject all except those whose trace prints were coded to activate the mechanism, but it would still be worth a try if he could manage to reach it. The main thing was to keep this madman talking. "Where have all these kids come from?" he asked.

"Kerala for the most part," replied Magobion. "Some from Madras and Pradesh."

"Lynn wasn't Indian."

"Lynn?"

"The girl Manders called Catherine."

"Mr. Linton, I confess that even now you still contrive to astonish me. How on earth did you discover her real name?"

"In the same way that I found out about *Kállos*. By asking questions."

"And what else did you learn about her?"

Laurie began inching his way toward the plate. "Quite a lot of interesting things, actually," he said. "Enough to lead us here, anyway."

"That was indeed unfortunte," agreed the Colonel. "Miss Scott had a very minor role in the research project and was simply the victim of her own insatiable appetite for sensation. As soon as I discovered what she was doing I took immediate steps to rectify the situation. Unfortunately she got wind of my suspicions and elected to take matters into her own hands. She prevailed upon one of the guards to ferry her to Tilbury during the course of which she apparently fell overboard from the hovercraft. At the time this seemed an eminently satisfactory conclusion to an otherwise wholly unsatisfactory episode but, as you will by now have realized, *Kállos* endows its devotees with quite exceptional powers. It was these, I now know, which enabled her to survive what would otherwise have been death and, incidentally, to set in train the unfortunate series of events of which today has witnessed the culmination."

Laurie's left hand was now only inches from the plate. "What did you do with her when you got her back? Kill her?"

"On the contrary," replied Magobion. "She is at present peacefully asleep in Module 32. I regret, however, that it will not be possible for me to introduce her. Come, Miss Kennedy, you will find that you are now free to move. I shall escort you personally to the guardroom. You, Mr. Linton, will remain here until I return."

Laurie watched the two of them move away down the tunnel and vanish into a concealed exit. The moment they disappeared from his view his questing fingertips brushed the rim of the plate they had been seeking. Just as he was about to attempt the switch he found his outstretched arm being pressed down, gently but firmly against his side and himself sliding back to the point from which he had started out. At that moment he felt like a small child who had been rebuked for misbehavior. In different circumstances his impotent frustration would have seemed almost comical.

For some moments he just stood there with his back pressed to the door, gazing down the tunnel and wondering dismally what Magobion would do with him. He suspected that whatever it was it would be both painful and prolonged. The old man was obviously a quintessential megalomaniac. But what if the powers he claimed to control proved to be not fantasy but fact? Would he not feel compelled to unleash them on the world simply to prove his own omnipotence? The thought bathed Laurie in a sweat of panic. "He's *insane!*" he cried out to the silent denizens of the womb-like cells. "Can't you understand that?"

"Laurie?"

The hair rose bristling on Laurie's scalp. The voice seemed to be coming from inside his own head. "C-Carol?" he stuttered.

"Don't you remember me?" whispered the seashell voice. '*You came to see me in the hospital."*

"Lynn?"

"You haven't forgotten then. What are you doing here?"

The situation was infinitely more fantastic than any dream he had ever dreamed. Pinned to the wall like a lepidopterist's specimen by some unknown, invisible force, scarcely able to move hand or foot, and yet able to "talk" with a girl who was lying in a drug-induced coma fifty yards away. "I'm waiting to be killed!" he wailed. *"By you!"*

"That's impossible," came the faint reply. *"We couldn't kill you. You're b'hoot."*

"?"

"B'hoot," repeated the voice patiently. *"Didn't you know?"*

"Know *what?*" he pleaded.

"That you're protected. You're the first we've seen."

Laurie closed his eyes and opened them. "He said you'd pull me to bits."

"*Oh, he doesn't realize.*" The voice was thin and tiny, clear and yet remote, like an insect singing in the throat of a flower. "*You're not really in our time at all. Not yet. You're part of yesterday or tomorrow. You're b'hoot.*"

What she was saying was the purest nonsense, and yet, in a weird and impossible way, perhaps it wasn't. Not altogether. "Can *he* kill me?" he said.

"*We're not sure. We think you're each other's threshold.*"

"What does that mean?"

"*Into our time,*" she said. "*And out of it.*"

"Let me out of here, Lynn."

"*It's not me, Laurie. It's them. They're afraid of you.*"

"But I won't hurt *them!* You know that. If Magobion isn't stopped we'll *all* be finished."

"*Then tell them so.*"

"How can I?"

"*Think it to them. In pictures. They'll understand.*"

So began the most extraordinary experience of Laurie's life—stranger even than the events of 1987—as, guided by Lynn's spectral voice he attempted to visualize some sort of sinister scenario in which Magobion set out to prove his dominion over the world. What he lacked in skill he made up for in desperation, and as one crudely outlined episode succeeded another he found himself becoming enmeshed in the web of his own fantasy. Watching the imaginary missiles lancing down like shooting stars from the twinkling spacestations, he was overwhelmed by the conviction that he was doing more than simply projecting a vision of some future Armageddon—that it was, himself, inextricably involved in preventing it! He believed that he was where he was, doing what he was doing, because he had somehow *chosen to be there;* that he was, in truth, what Lynn had called him—"Part of tomorrow." As the boiling, blood-colored clouds spewed upward and the radioactive gruel of death descended like gray snow upon the innocent and the guilty alike, he felt the restraining pressure on his body suddenly relax and he staggered forward down the aisle of the tunnel.

"Well?" he panted. "Now what?"

"They want to know what will happen to them if they help you to escape. Will they be able to stay as they are? That's all they ask, Laurie. To be left to dream in peace."

Laurie moved along the cells hunting for Lynn. He found her at the far end of the right hand row. She was lying just as she had lain when he had first seen her in the Rehabilitation Center, except that this time she was naked and her eyes were closed. Once again he found himself recalling Manders phrase: *"the pot of gold at the rainbow's end."* "Is that what you want too?" he asked.

The hydro-mattress slowly humped itself up and rolled her on to her other side. *"What else have you to offer?"*

"There's life, Lynn. And other people. There's love."

"There's death. And other people. And hate," she replied with a ghostly chuckle. *"And for these kids there's slow starvation and grinding poverty and every sort of hideous illness too. Nothing you could offer them outside would compare with what we've got now. Don't feel sorry for us, Laurie. Doctor Manders was right. We're hooked on Paradise."*

"And when Magobion decides to end it all? What then?"

"We won't let him."

154

"How could you stop him?"

"We do what he wants because he gives us our Kállos. Convince us that we'll go on getting it and Magobion can go to hell."

"Oh, you'll still get it all right," sighed Laurie. "Haven't you kids realized that potentially you're the most powerful weapon in the whole world? Every government will be falling over itself to have its own battery of dreamers. The only way of defusing you is to do what they did with the atom bomb— spread the secret around so that everyone gets a share. Who knows? it might even persuade the military idiots to dismantle their doomsday machines. Can't you tell your friends that?"

"All right," she said. *"I'll try."*

He was still waiting for her answer when the door at the far end of the tunnel purred open and he saw the Colonel silhouetted against the slicing light from the distant landing. There was nobody with him.

"Well, now, Mr. Linton, it's time for us . . ." The confident sentence broke off as he realized that Laurie was no longer standing where he had left him. He said something in rapid dialect. The doors closed behind him.

"You must go now," whispered Lynn's voice. *"They're going to help you and the girl to get away, but that's all. They won't risk harming the old man."*

As she said this Laurie felt himself being lifted bodily and carried down the tunnel into the exit niche through which he had previously seen Carol vanish with Magobion. A door slid open and he found himself standing at the top of another spiral flow-away. As the door murmured shut behind him and the floor began slowly swirling him down to the story below he heard the fading whisper of Lynn's voice wishing him *"Good luck"* and then, so faint and far away he almost doubted whether he had heard it, *"Remember you're b'hoot."*

The flow-way deposited him at the entrance to a storeroom. He glanced around cautiously, saw that it was deserted, and then realized that the metal shelves were all neatly stacked with row upon row of cardboard cartons, each one of which bore a monogrammed *K&S* label. He noticed a box which had already been opened, helped himself to a handful of the ampoules it contained and stuffed them into his pocket. Then he sauntered nonchalantly out into an adjoining control room.

The only occupant was an overalled technician who was scrutinizing a computer print-out. He glanced up questioningly as Laurie entered, then, as Laurie gave him a friendly nod, he nodded back and returned his attention to his work. A minute later Laurie discovered a side-exit that was standing open and stepped out into the compound.

At every moment he expected to hear the wailing of an alarm siren but nothing happened and he broke into a gentle trot toward the guardhouse, breathing a silent prayer that somehow Lynn could contrive to keep her word.

Their car was standing just where he had left it and there was no sign of a guard anywhere. The absence of any sort of activity was almost uncanny. He imagined Sergeant Rogers squinting at him pensively down the sights of a high-powered rifle and expected every second to experience the outrageous agony of an explosive bullet in his stomach. None came. He jogged on up to the guardhouse, twisted the handle and stepped inside.

The first thing he saw was the plastic sole of a military boot protruding from beneath an up-turned table. The silence everywhere was almost palpable.

What could have happened? "Carol?" he called fearfully. "Carol?"

There was a muffled cry from behind a door at the far side of the room. He dodged around the table and thrust the door open.

Carol was lying slumped back in a chair. Her face was as white as if it had been dusted with chalk. Sprawled on the floor at her feet, his head grotesquely twisted so that it was looking directly backward over his shoulders, was Sergeant Rogers. His eyes were so wide open that a rim of white was clear all around each iris, and the expression of absolute terror on his dead face almost stopped Laurie's heart. *"Jesus Christ!"* he whispered. "What happened?"

Carol reached out toward him and wailed like a baby.

He hauled her to her feet and dragged her stumbling behind him back into the guardroom. "We've got to get those gates open," he said. "How do they work them?"

His glance darted around the room and found the lever switch he was seeking. He lunged forward and wrenched it down. The compound gates swung open with a crash that jarred the building to its foundations.

"Come on!" he cried, and was about to drag her out when he caught sight of his gun lying on the floor in a corner of the room. He picked it up, thrust it back into its holster, and hustled Carol outside.

He could feel her shaking under his hand as he steered her across the twenty yards of asphalt separating them from the car, snatched open the door and bundled her inside. Then he raced around to the other side and clambered in.

The engine started at the first twist of the key. He risked a last glance back and saw the compound was as deserted as he had ever seen it. The car rolled forward through the gates and down on to the causeway. He stamped down hard on the accelerator and they howled up through the gears till the reeds on either side had merged into a rippling blur.

They covered the two miles to the outer gate in about ninety seconds. Even so Laurie was beginning to wonder if they would ever reach it. Yet they were through it and half a mile on down the road beyond before he heard, faint in the distance behind them, the thin wailing of an alarm siren. His mind flicked into overdrive. "The skyport, Caro! They'll block off the control at Dagenham. Here . . ." He groped in his pocket and thrust four of the precious ampoules into her lap. "We'll have to split up at Maplin. You've got to get those to Martell somehow. It's our only chance. Blow the secret wide open. I'll try and contact Gross—tell him everything I can. God knows what he'll make of it—Oh Christ!" He dragged the wheel hard over and slung the Ford into a juddering, four-wheel slide which carried them halfway up the bank and just past an oncoming delivery van. They had a fleeting glimpse of the driver's ashen face and then they had rocked back on to the road again and were roaring through Ockenford.

What had taken them fifteen minutes coming took them scarcely five on the way back. Luckily there was little traffic on the secondaries. When they gained the feeder road for the M501 Laurie swung right into the east-bound lanes. "What happened back there in the guardhouse?" he said. "Or can't you talk about it?"

Carol shuddered. "That man Rogers was just starting to question me. Magobion had told him we were spies. Rogers wasn't working me over or anything, just asking questions. And then—" she made a sudden grab for the window lever and just managed to get her face outside.

"Christ," murmured Laurie reverently. "It was that bad, was it?"

She nodded and retched drily. "His head just

seemed to be twisting around," she gulped. "Like winding a watch . . . and there was a noise like wood splintering . . . The next thing I remember is hearing you calling me."

"Magobion wasn't kidding, was he?" he muttered and then sketched in the rough outlines of his own part in the affair. "But they won't touch him," he concluded, "and there was nothing I could think of to persuade them. God knows why I didn't do the job while I had the chance."

"Could you?"

"Not that way," he said. "Not even to him. When it came to it I just couldn't hate him enough. They seem to have picked the wrong one in me."

"What do you mean?"

"*You* know what I mean—Billie!"

"You don't still believe *that!*"

"More than ever," he said. "I think it's why those kids didn't kill me back there. Lynn said something I couldn't understand. She told me I was *b'hoot*—protected."

"*Protected?* How?"

"I wish I knew. But if I *was* right the other night, Caro—when you told me I was 'high,' remember?—then what she said *could* make a sort of sense. If we —you and I—could have known what we know now *but known it five years ago!* We could maybe have forestalled Magobion somehow—warned Strübe or something—anyway we could have tried to prevent this happening."

"But we didn't, Laurie."

"I *know* we didn't. But don't you *see,* Caro? What we're doing *now,* we're doing *because of what happened to me in 1987!* No one *ordered* us to go to Geneva. There was no real *reason* why we had to come *back* when we did. No one even ordered us to come back here today. Yet we *did.* Whenever

159

there's been a fork in the road I've *always* taken the one which would lead me to Magobion."

"Yet you didn't kill him when you had the chance."

"No," he said. "No, I didn't kill him."

"So the whole theory breaks down."

"Maybe," he said. "Or maybe the 'killing' was just figurative. Politically speaking, if we can manage to blow *Kállos*, we'll kill Magobion stone dead." As he spoke his eyes flicked up to the mirror. He frowned. "That Lancer's been on our tail since before we hit the motorway."

Carol swiveled in her seat. "Are you sure?"

"Almost positive. It came up just after we were through Ockenford."

"*Could* it be them? Already?"

"I shouldn't have thought so. Anyway they could have overtaken us if they'd wanted to. Those jet-jobs can do over a hundred and thirty."

They flashed under the span sign that warned them they were approaching the skyport and saw the spindly tracery of the mono-rail viaduct flickering in on a long silvery curve from their left. Laurie coaxed the Ford over into the appropriate lane and scanned the mirror anxiously. "I was right," he muttered. "Here they come. Now listen, Caro. You've got to grab yourself a seat on anything you can get—Europe, Scandinavia, anywhere. At the first touch-down, change planes and double back to Paris. Whatever happens *you've got to get that stuff to Martell!* Tell him everything you know; beg him to do a break-down analysis; and then make him *broadcast his results world-wide!* Tell him that there's every chance humanity's hanging on it. He'll get the point."

Carol nodded. "And what will you do?"

"Like I said. Try and contact Gross. But the vital thing is to get you away. I'll go through the tunnel and into the cab bay. As soon as you're out I'll carry

160

on around and head back toward London. If I'm dead lucky they'll follow me. I'll aim for Harwich or somewhere. That should give you the break you need."

"And if they catch you?"

Laurie smiled grimly. "Then I guess it'll all be up to Lynn."

As they approached the mouth of the tunnel they had a stroke of good fortune. The control lights changed and by gunning the Ford Laurie just managed to squeeze through on the last flicker of the amber. Two other cars blocked the tailing Lancer. The sixty seconds' grace Laurie gained gave him just the margin he needed to drop Carol off at the terminal and pull away into the stream of vehicles leaving the airport.

But as he re-emerged from the access tunnel he discovered that his meager supply of luck had already run out. Heading down the approach road toward him, sirens screeching, were two black and red M.I.S. patrol trucks. They spotted the Ford at the same instant and flashed their lights imperiously.

Laurie ducked, swung the wheel hard over to the left, crashed through the flimsy wooden fencing separating him from the perimeter track and, trailing splintered debris, hurtled back beneath the monorail pylons toward the terminal building.

The audacity of the maneuver caught the M.I.S. drivers by surprise. By the time one of them had succeeded in forcing his truck through the oncoming traffic, Laurie had reached the sanctuary of the terminal, abandoned the Ford and vanished into the crowd.

Unfamiliar though he was with the layout of the Maplin skyport, Laurie had no difficulty in finding the video-phone booths. He squeezed his way into one and dialed the Windsor NARCOS number. Within seconds the screen had cleared and he was face to face with Major Gross's secretary. "Why, hello, Mr. Linton," she smiled. "Where are you calling fr—" and then the line died.

Laurie swore savagely and re-dialed. This time nothing happened at all. He counted up to ten, buzzed for the operator, and when she appeared gave her the number. The screen jigged and flickered. Thirty seconds later she said: "Where are you calling from, sir?"

"Maplin," he replied. "It's an International Credit Rating Call. Urgent."

"One moment, sir. Hold the line please."

Laurie pressed his forehead against the screen and screamed silently. A moment later he heard the relay speakers boom: *Attention all travelers! Attention all travelers! This is an International Security alert! You are warned to be on the look out for a young man in blue NARCOS uniform. This man is dangerous! Report his whereabouts to any Security Guard or the skyport police.*

Before the announcement had ended Laurie had dropped the phone receiver back in its cradle, ripped the telltale insignia from his lapels and thrust them into his pockets. He was baffled by the fact that there had been no mention of Carol even though the two men in the Lancer must have seen her.

He backed out of the booth, strode boldly across the busy main hall of the terminal and into the skyport Post Office. Having purchased a registered envelope he addressed it to Major Gross, wrapped up four of the K-12 ampoules in telegram forms, stuffed them into the envelope with a scribbled note of explanation and posted it. As far as he could judge nobody paid him the slightest attention.

There was a broadcast announcement about a flight departing for Rome and another to Geneva. He

162

prayed that Carol had managed to get herself aboard one of them. He took another telegram form, sauntered across to the long shelf-desk behind the window and positioned himself so that he had a clear view across the main hall to the entrance of the terminal. The security alert was repeated over the relay system —still with no mention of Carol.

He saw four armed M.I.S. men take up stations at the exits and start scanning the hurrying crowds.

An elderly man came over and knocked out his pipe into the ash bin beside Laurie. "What's all the fuss about?" he asked.

Laurie shrugged. "Some V.I.P. arriving, I suppose."

The man grunted sardonically. "More of our bloody taxes down the drain, eh?"

Laurie grinned briefly, took out his pen and made a pretense of drafting his telegram. Now and again he glanced up as if seeking inspiration. In the space of five minutes he counted eleven M.I.S. guards, all armed, and at least a dozen skyport police. More were coming in all the time.

A group of students staggering under enormous ruck-sacks were assembling around the entrance to the Post Office. Seizing his chance, Laurie hurried out and edged his way among them. A minute later as a high-piled baggage floater hissed past, he fell into step beside it and, using it as a screen, headed purposefully toward the mono-rail flow-ways.

He had covered scarcely half the distance when he realized his mistake. At each flow-way access port an M.I.S. guard and a police constable had been stationed to scan the passengers who were being carried up toward the mono-rail platforms. He glanced back over his shoulder and was just in time to see the guards at the main entrance snap to attention in a rigid salute. A moment later Colonel Magobion strode into the terminal accompanied by a police Superintendent.

The baggage floater reached the flow-ways and swung off toward the Customs check-point. As it did so the policeman nearest to Laurie caught sight of the Superintendent and the Colonel. He called out to his M.I.S. companion and they both turned their heads and gazed across toward the terminal entrance.

Laurie was aboard the pavement, bending down and fiddling with his shoe buckle, almost before he himself realized it. Two seconds later he was past the checkpoint and gliding up toward the mono-rail bays forty feet above the floor of the terminal.

He was over halfway up the long incline when the loudspeakers crackled and a man's voice boomed: *"Attention Security forces! Monitor identification lane 5! Check! Hold land 5!"*

Laurie became nakedly conscious of hundreds of curious faces turning toward them from adjoining flow-ways. The woman immediately in front of him cried excitedly: "Why, isn't that *us?*" and craned her head around to peer back down the track. She gazed right at Laurie but did not notice him.

"Hold Lane 5!" came the repeated command. "All *flow-way passengers remain in their places!"*

The track began to slow perceptibly.

"Do not move!"

Beyond the trellis barrier immediately to his left Laurie saw that the baggage lanes were still functioning normally. Thirty yards back down the slope the M.I.S. guard had quit his station at the access point and was squeezing his way up the track peering at the passengers.

"Oh *my!*" gurgled Laurie's neighbor. "Isn't this just too exc*it*ing?"

The flow-way stopped altogether.

"Excuse me," muttered Laurie and slipped past the peering woman.

"Look! That's him!" called a child's shrill voice from the adjoining track. "He's got a blue uniform!"

Laurie broke into a shuffling run up the incline, dodging around astonished passengers, most of whom just gaped stupidly, or pulled away from him as though he had the plague.

"*Stay where you are, Linton!*" yelled the loud-speakers. "*Positive identification confirmed! Lane 5! Lane 5!*"

A group of airforce cadets bunched together and blocked his way. Below him whistles shrilled. He vaulted over the barrier and leaped for the baggage lane as a rifle cracked and a bullet ricocheted off a metal stanchion and hummed up toward the roof like an angry bee. He gained the flow-way, stumbled and fell flat. A second bullet whucked into a suitcase within inches of his head.

He rolled over, snatched the Semling from its holster and, scrabbling to his feet, sprinted the twenty yards to the mono-rail deck and dived behind the waist-high parapet.

He had no plan at all unless it was to hold them off for as long as possible. He knew there was no escape just as surely as he knew that Magobion would be satisfied with nothing less than his dead body. But this knowledge filled him not so much with fear as with a curious kind of ice-cold fury which bordered almost upon exultation.

Bent double he scuttled crab-wise along behind the parapet and gained the cover of the huge "Arrival and Departure" indicator which was braced out a few feet in front of the barrier by a series of latticed alloy struts. From this vantage point he risked a peep downward and saw that the center of the vast hallway had been swept clear of people as though by a gigantic broom. They were huddled around the sides of the terminal, their faces turned up toward him, a thousand anonymous dots of human confetti.

Close beside him a loudspeaker bawled: *"Attention Security! Linton now concealed behind upper deck parapet! Co-ordinate to secure!"*

Glancing up, Laurie saw the predatory beak of a remote-controlled monitor camera perched on a high gantry, come jerking around in quest of him.

Resting the barrel of the Semling on the rim of the parapet he took deliberate aim at the lens, fired twice, and missed with both shots. Nevertheless one bullet must have nicked some vital hydraulic artery because the camera slowly drooped as though its neck was broken and a thin thread of emerald green liquid began to waver downward.

Immediately, a fusilade of shots smashed through the indicator. One of them ripped out a long splinter, leaving a narrow slit which afforded him an almost perfect view of the whole arena. His first glimpse revealed that the guard who had been clambering up the stationary flow-way had got to within ten yards of the parapet. Aiming deliberately low, Laurie fired and saw the man drop his gun and clutch at his thigh. In so doing he lost his balance, toppled backward and rolled away down the long slope between the pavements.

In immediate response half a dozen more shots crashed into the indicator which now began to fizzle and throw off angry violet sparks. Laurie thrust a fresh clip into the Semling and, risking electrocution, took another peep through the crack. Some sort of tactical conference appeared to be going on down below. He could see Magobion and the Superintendent talking to two of the guards who then doubled away to left and right and passed out of his view. He found himself wondering in an oddly detached sort of way what it would feel like to die, and from there his mind flickered back to Lynn and the dreamers where it hovered doubtfully for a moment before fluttering off to himself as a boy and to Carol who was yet Billie and had dreamed a dying dream. Could Time really be turned inside out like an old sock so that yesterday was beyond tomorrow? "Who are you, Laurie Linton?" he murmured. "Do you really exist?"

The words were still on his lips when two gas grenades lobbed up and burst like rotten-ripe pears within ten feet of where he was crouched.

He realized that he had at last traveled this road to the very end but, even so, some mulish instinct still drove him to suck in one last huge gulp of clear air and, having done so, to squirm over the top of the parapet on to one of the metal struts of the indicator panel.

He clung there while the choking tendrils writhed toward him and his eyes began to sting and blur, but a current of air was funneled up between the parapet and the board and though, from below, it was quite obvious that no one could possibly survive the poisonous cloud that is exactly what he did.

Three minutes later as they moved in confidently to take him he pushed the muzzle of the Semling through the narrow crack, blinked the tears from his smarting eyes, waited until he dared wait no more and fired just two shots. One struck Colonel Magobion in the left eye; the other hit him in the chest. He died without ever knowing how it had happened.

In the savage pandemonium of firing which followed Laurie too was hit twice, once in the right shoulder and once in the left forearm. As a direct result he lost his grip on the stanchion, fell forty feet in a fraction over one second and was still conscious when he reached the ground.

During that single interminable second he knew the

167

peace that passeth all understanding and was happier than he had ever been. The last thing he remembered was hearing the seashell whisper of a girl's voice saying: *"b'hoot."*

As Carol stepped out of the expressavator capsule on the 57th floor of the Barbican Intensive Care Unit she caught sight of a uniformed police sergeant and walked down the daylit corridor toward him. He glanced at the identity pass she held out to him and his expression altered. "Oh, so you're the Miss Kennedy we've been hearing so much about," he said with a smile. "It's a privilege to meet you, Miss."

"I bet you wouldn't have said that a week ago, Sergeant."

"Ah, well," said the Sergeant and shrugged, conceding the point.

"I can go in?"

"Carry on, Miss."

She knocked on the door and without waiting for a reply, depressed the lever handle and walked in.

Laurie was sitting up in bed savoring a blush-making account of himself in an illustrated journal. He was naked to the waist and his right shoulder and his left forearm were swathed in what looked like gold foil. Two enormous black eyes gave him a remarkable resemblance to a racoon. "Caro!" he cried delightedly, flinging the paper to one side. "I wasn't expecting you till tomorrow!"

She ran to him, leaned down and gave him a long, open-mouthed kiss that did nothing to improve his pulse rate. "Didn't you get my videogram?"

"Yes, it's here somewhere," he said, groping around in the wild jumble of letters and newspapers that littered the bed and spilled over on to the floor. "It's been a real madhouse these last three days."

168

"I can imagine. How do you feel now?"

"Half drunk most of the time. They're taking this lot off on Sunday."

"I saw you on Euro So-Vi."

"Did you recognize me?"

"Just." She laughed. "I can see why you wore the dark glasses though."

"Aren't they a pair of beauties? The old M.I.S. plastic boot must pack quite a punch. Not that I knew a thing about it at the time. Just as well, maybe."

Carol scooped up an armful of letters, dropped them on the floor, and sat herself down on the side of the bed. "Well, where do you want me to start?" she said.

"Better make it the beginning. When you scooted into the terminal."

She nodded. "Well, I hared straight for the flight office and found there were two flights due out in the next fifteen minutes. I tried for the Rome one first but they wouldn't let me have a Credit seat and I hadn't enough cash to buy an ordinary one so I had to settle for Geneva. That turned out to be a real stroke of luck in the end, but I'll explain that in a moment.

"Anyway I grabbed my boarding ticket and rushed off to the Departures bay. I wasn't looking to see if I was being followed, I was just desperate to get on board that plane. You'll never know how relieved I felt when I eventually sank down into my seat.

"I heard the broadcast announcement about you just before they closed the doors and I don't think I've ever come much closer to passing out. I was so sure you were on your way to Harwich. I just crossed my fingers and prayed. There wasn't anything else I could do. I was positive that they'd hold back the flight. But they didn't. I looked back as we took off, but the fact is I could hardly see a thing because I was crying.

"When we got over the Channel I went into the toilet. I was worried stiff about those K-12 ampoules. Then I remembered what we call a girl's advantage and slipped two of them in you-know-where.

"It's just as well I did because I'd no sooner got back to my place than a man came and sat himself down in the seat next to me. At first I assumed he was just another prowling wolf and I was all prepared to give him my special anti-wolf treatment when he said: 'Mam'selle Kennedy, I believe.'

"Talk about going into free-fall! When I found I could speak again I asked him who he was. 'I am a business associate of M'sieur Benoit,' he said. 'I have followed you and M'sieur Linton to the skyport. I suspect you may be in possession of a certain piece of property which would be of great interest to *Mondiale*.'

"Well it was pretty obvious that he wasn't the type to take 'no' for an answer so I told him that I was just on my way to see Benoit. That's what I meant when I said the Geneva flight was a lucky break. I don't know whether he believed me, but he made it very clear that he wasn't going to let me out of his sight, just in case I might feel like changing my mind. And he stuck to me like a plaster right up to the moment he ushered me into Benoit's office."

At that point Carol paused and eyed Laurie apprehensively.

"Well, go on," he said. "Don't keep me in suspense. What happened?"

Instead of answering she unzipped her handbag, took out a long blue envelope and laid it on the sheet beside him.

"What's that?" he asked.

"It's for you."

"From *Benoit?*"

She nodded. "Go on. Open it."

Laurie fumbled the envelope open and shook out four crisp new currency bills. Each was for ten thousand Swiss francs. He stared at them incredulously. "Oh, no," he groaned. "I don't believe it."

"They're real, Laurie."

He picked one up, turned it over between his fingers, and then began to chuckle. Within seconds they were both leaning helplessly against each other howling with hysterical laughter.

When eventually Laurie began to sober down he fisted the tears from his cheeks and groped around on the bed till he found that morning's copy of *The Telegraph.* "Just listen to this!" he gasped. " '*The announcement from Paris yesterday evening by Professor Henri Martell that he has succeeded in manufacturing the psychodrug known as 'Kállos-12,' coming together with the publication of his results, adds a somewhat ironic footnote to the events which have occupied the world's headliners for the past five days*' . . ."

It was no use, Laurie was laughing too much to go on.

"What wouldn't I have given to see Gabriel's face today?" gurgled Carol. "Do you suppose he'll write it off to research expenses?"

"I don't imagine he'd even miss it," said Laurie. "You know Martell sent a message about me to the P.M.?"

She nodded. "Did it help?"

"Gross seemed to think it might even have tipped the balance. After all it came right on top of the Peking resolution and the NARCOS petition. You know they've convened a Special Commission of Investigation?"

"No," said Carol. "What's that?"

"Four M.P.'s—two Government and two Opposition—and a legal boffin from the Home Office. They all trooped in to see me this morning and grilled me for over two hours. When it was over they all queued up and shook me solemnly by the hand. It was quite a touching little scene."

"Are they still going to arraign you?"

"They wouldn't say. It's up to Parliament apparently. There was a lot of airy-fairy chat about what constitutes high treason. They even suggested I might have to apply for a royal pardon. You know treason still carries the death penalty?"

"They wouldn't dare!" Carol averred stoutly.

Laurie grinned. "Between you and me I'm inclined to agree with you. What they're looking for is a way out without losing too much face. They know it's not a national thing any longer. There's a long telegram from Delhi down there somewhere saying they're going to raise the whole matter before the U.N. General Assembly and offering me the freedom of Kerala or somewhere. According to *Le Monde* the *force de frappe* is now as *passé* as trench warfare, and for once the Americans and the Russians seem to agree with them. But Fleet Street beats the lot! Last week you'd have thought I was Klaus Fuchs, Burgess, Blake and McLean all rolled into one. Killing Magobion was the most infamous act of treachery since Guy Fawkes. Now it seems all that was a misunderstanding. So exit Public Enemy, enter International Hero. I tell you, Caro, you see before you the biggest P.R. resurrection job since Lazarus."

"You wait," laughed Carol. "They're probably planning to have you publicly beheaded on Tower Hill."

"Not me. I'm *b'hoot*."

"You're *what?*"

"*B'hoot*. Have you forgotten? It's what Lynn called me."

172

"What's it mean?"

"I only found out yesterday. It means 'ghost' in Hindi. One of the nurses told me. As far as I'm concerned it's what allows you to be shot full of holes and then fall forty feet on to reinforced concrete without even a bruise to show for it. If that isn't enough to prevent a simple thing like having my head chopped off then nothing is."

Carol shook her own head in mock despair and then said: "Oh, by the way, I asked Henri about that stuff *prozatamine*. You remember? The drug which was supposed to let you jump backward in Time."

"Oh, yes. What about it?"

"It never even got off the ground. Jean Roland, the genius who dreamed it up went and got himself killed last year in a road accident."

"Last *year!* You're sure you don't mean nine years ago?"

"Last year," she repeated firmly.

Laurie sighed philosophically. "So yet another beautiful hypothesis bites the dust. Too bad."

Carol nodded. "There was *one* rather odd thing though," she said. "I'm not sure whether I ought to tell you."

Laurie growled threateningly.

"What would you say if I told you that Roland dropped right out of scientific research in 1987?"

Laurie opened his mouth and then closed it again without saying anything.

"He cleared off and joined some weird religious sect in Ceylon." She pursed up her lips teasingly. "Do I need to tell you the month?"

Still Laurie said nothing.

"Don't you believe me?"

He laid his head back on his pillows and closed his bruised eyes. "Oh, *I* believe you, all right," he said. "But no one else ever will. No one."

173

"Are you sure *you* do?" she asked with a smile.

He opened his eyes and looked up at her. "I *know* it's true, Caro," he said. "And I'll tell you *how* I know. After they'd shot that gas up at me and I saw Magobion starting to walk toward me I stuck my gun through the crack *but I didn't point it at him!* I aimed at a place ten feet in front of him *and four yards to the left!* I simply held it there and waited. And instead of coming straight on as he should have done, *he moved across to his right!* When I pulled that trigger I *knew* he was already dead. And when I fell it was as though I was falling out of a dream I'd already dreamed. It was what I'd seen over my own shoulder all those years ago—the thing I couldn't remember. *It was what I had to do!*"

"So you still think they sent you back to kill him?"

"I do, yes. Or sent me *on* to do it."

"But for all we know Magobion might never have done anything."

"Perhaps not here—to *us*. But there, where that other Laurie came from, things must have been different. After all, we both know Magobion was as mad as a hatter. Perhaps in their time he was just too big a risk altogether and so they had to get rid of *him* by getting in touch with *me*."

"If they ever did," murmured Carol.

"Oh, they did, Caro. And it worked."

"For *us,* maybe," she said.

The door opened and a pretty little Indian nurse came in dragging a gleaming trolley on which was mounted a large U.V. lamp. "Time for your sunbathe, Mr. B'hoot," she grinned.

Carol stood up, retrieved her handbag, and then picked up the four currency bills. "And these?" she asked.

"A generous donàtion from *Mondiale* to the Linton-Kennedy Appeal Fund?" suggested Laurie.

"Or the Magobion Memorial Fund?" countered Carol.

"If there's a point where charity becomes hypocrisy," said Laurie, "then as far as I'm concerned that would be it."

Carol laughed. "Could it be that you're biased?" she said.